Snapdragon:

And Six More Stories with Bite

Jack Kardiac

Snapdragon: *And Six More Short Stories with Bite*

Copyright © 2014 Jack Kardiac

Published by Mills Creative Minds, LLC, Lubbock TX

This title is also available as an ebook. Visit www.JacKardiac.com.

Disclaimer: The persons, places, things, and otherwise animate or inanimate objects mentioned in this novel are figments of the author's imagination. Any resemblance to anything or anyone living (or dead) is unintentional. The author humbly begs your pardon. This is a work of fiction, people.

Cover design: Mills Creative Minds, LLC

Printed in the United States of America

ISBN-13: 978-0-9833533-8-6

ISBN-10: 0-9833533-8-6

CONTENTS

ACKNOWLEDGMENTS

As with any great achievement in life, this was not a solo project by any stretch of the imagination. There are a handful of people who helped make *Snapdragon* happen, and here's where they finally get the recognition they deserve.

First and foremost, my wife **Kim**. Your encouragement, support and long nights reading and rereading my drafts gave the confidence (delusion?) that I needed to plow through. You're the best wife / mother / editor I could have ever hoped for. I love you!

Secondly, my beta readers. These are the ones who glanced through my second drafts and told me what rocks, what stinks and what I can do to make the stories shine. In completely random order (because that just seems fair):

Abby Goldsmith	Jenny Flake Rabe
Amy Edwards	Elly Green
Jack de Nileth	Kate Gorman
Melissa Gaines	Logan Pickell
Er-Yearn Jang	Ashley Clarke
Dawn S. Toles	David Seow

You are the most fantastic people ever, taking the time to read through the early drafts of these stories and seeing the potential they held beneath their rough exteriors. Your suggestions and comments had a huge impact on the flow and readability of each and every story.

Thirdly, my editors Lisa Moise and Michelle Coppens. Your attention to detail and professional polishing are invaluable. May no one else discover how truly talented you are. Of course, it goes without saying that any remaining errors and mistakes are mine and mine alone.

Lastly, I want to thank *you*, dear reader, for simply being here. Every single day, you have an endless array of entertainment options at your disposal. Thank you for choosing to read my stories instead. I'm extremely grateful for your time, and I will promise you this about *Snapdragon* — you may be shocked, disgusted or amused by what you're about to read, but you most definitely will not be bored.

-Jack

ORANGE, BLACK AND BLUE

"I hate Florida."

Mitch looks up at me, startled. "Crud, Billy! You almost made me crap my pants!" He frowns at me. "How long you been standing there?" Reaching across the bench, he casually picks up the orange that's been sitting beside him for the past fifteen minutes.

"Long enough," I say.

He shrugs. "So I guess this is it, huh?"

"Yeah, it is," I say, slapping yet another mosquito trying to burrow into the back of my neck. "Man! These things are *everywhere*! I'm dyin' down here!"

"Can't take the heat, huh?"

"Excuse me?"

"Better'n Vegas, that's for sure," he says, frowning. "That place is messed up."

I stare at him, sizing him up. "So, level with me. Why'd you do it? I mean, you seriously thought you could steal sixty-seven thousand and skip town?"

"Sixty-five."

"Whatever."

He shrugs again, staring out across the bay. "Had to try."

I shake my head. "Mitch. You're not some hotshot, big league pitcher anymore. You're done. A has-been whose only play left is pitching money

2

away on sorry bets."

"Says you," he mumbles, tossing the orange between his hands. He's obviously hurt. Or angry. Or both.

"Says me? Buddy, I been watching you for a week down here. Everyday it's the same. You sleep all day, eat a sub from the corner shop an' then come down here with your two freaking oranges to watch the sunset."

"So?"

"Every. Single. Night."

"So what?" he says, sounding irritated.

"So what? Don't you see? Mitch. You're pathetic. A washed-up belly-itcher who screwed with the wrong guys, an' now they sent me to clean up your sorry mess."

Mitch nods, but says nothing.

"So where is it?"

"Where's what?"

"Where's…" I shake my head, exasperated. "The *money*, you moron!"

He shrugs. "Spent it."

"Where?"

"In Vegas. Where else?"

"All of it?"

"Pretty much," he says, then cocks his head. "Why? You want some?"

"Crap, Mitch. You really are a loser, you know that?"

"Well, that's what you keep telling me."

I stare at him and shake my head, sweat soaking a slick streak down the back of my shirt. "Look," I say, removing my knife from inside my jacket. "I'm not

3

sadistic or nothin'. I can make it quick. One deep cut and you'll bleed out. It'll feel like going to sleep or something."

He snickers. "Or something," he repeats quietly, shaking his head slowly. He stares out at the sun, still fiddling with the orange in his hands. "Guess everybody dies sometime," he says, getting up from the bench.

"Don't run…"

"I'm not gonna run…"

"Good, 'cause I'm not in the mood." I take a step forward and then pause. "There's one thing I gotta know first."

"Oh yeah? And what's that?" he says, frowning at the ground.

"What's with the other orange?"

He looks up at me, confused. "What?"

"The orange." I nod toward his hands. "Every single day I been watching you, an' every single day you come out here at sunset, sit on the bench and eat an orange. Then a half hour later you pitch the other one into the pond and walk away."

"You saw that, huh?"

"Yeah."

"So I like oranges…"

"Uh-huh."

"So what?"

"So, is it some kinda therapy or something? Somehow makes you feel better about your crap life?"

Mitch stares at me. "Look," he says finally, "I'll tell you the truth, but you're gonna have two problems."

"Such as?"

"One, you're not going to believe me."

"And two?"

"You won't like my answer."

A sneer flashes across my face. "Try me."

He suddenly flashes a grin at me, and a split-second too late I notice he's planted his feet. The look in his eye ratchets up from dejected to determined.

His arm cocks back and I know I'm in serious trouble.

"It's frozen," he says.

My left eye explodes as the iced orange pegs it dead center, shattering my skull. A thousand diamonds dance through my head, and as I hit the ground, fading fast, a singular, final thought shoots into the forefront of my mind.

I *really* hate Florida.

Author's Note

I *really* like writing short stories. Being able to take a random scene, character or snippet of dialogue and expanding it makes me smile and fills me with some kind of juvenile glee.

As I brushed up on my short story skills through reading the variety of "how-to" books and a good portion of Alfred Hitchcock anthologies, I began to study flash fiction a bit more. I subscribed to an ezine called *Shotgun Honey**, which publishes flash fiction stories in the vein of noir, crime and the like. Reading a handful of tightly-crafted, satisfying stories tends to inspire me.

So I sat down and wrote one myself. Short, sweet, and to-the-point. Loved the concept, loved the end result and loved the story. (Hope you did, too!)

*I actually submitted my story to Shotgun Honey when I was done, and they liked it enough to feature it on their website. A serious highlight for this budding author.

MODEL PET

"Please don't kill my cat."

I look up from the TV and stare at her. "What?"

Megan stares back at me, frowning. "I'm serious, Jason. I'm only going to be gone for two days. That's it. It's a huge favor, I know…"

"Wait. Slow down. Now, what are we talking about again?" I attempt to give her my full attention, but my eyes dart back to the television. They're running yet another story about people's pets being stolen, or running away. I snicker inside. Third time this week, and the news department *still* can't settle on an angle.

"Jason!"

I jump in my chair. "What! I'm sorry… I'll do it!" I glance around the room, trying to uncover a clue or a hint to get me out of her crosshairs. I find none. "Okay… where are you going again?"

"Oh. My. *Word.*"

Megan sighs deeply and grabs her purse off the table, avoiding eye contact. "Never mind. This was a mistake…" She rises to leave, and I dart ahead of her, intercepting her at the door.

"No, wait, please. I'm sorry. *Seriously*, you can count on me, I just—" I shrug, looking as pathetic as I feel. "I… got distracted." She takes a step back and shakes her head, clearly upset, but I can see she's stifling a smirk. I still have a chance. "I'm sorry," I plead. "I want to help. I do. Please?"

"Fine," Megan says, crossing her arms. "Do I have your full attention this time?"

I stand erect and salute her. "Yes, ma'am, you do."

She grins. "No distractions?"

"None," I say, hitting the MUTE button on the remote.

"Okay, then."

She leans in closer, and I try not to let on how incredibly intoxicating her perfume is. "I'm leaving this afternoon for a two-day conference in Las Vegas. My sister Mandy was going to look after him, but she's sick, so…"

"…so you need me to watch your cat?"

"I know you're busy with your work and you're not really a pet lover, but it would seriously mean a lot to me."

"Ah, no worries," I wave her off and pray my charming grin hides the lie. "I love animals."

Megan raises a brow. "Is that so?"

I pray harder as I watch her eyes narrow. "Ahhhh-bsolutely. Love 'em. Love, love, love."

"Well…okay, then." She flashes a brilliant smile, and I try not to melt. "You've officially moved up to my new favorite neighbor."

"Sweet."

"And I promise I'll cook you some of my fettuccini alfredo for dinner when I come back. Deal?"

"Deal."

"But…" She holds up a warning finger, head cocked to the side. "It's not a date. Understand?"

"Of course not. Just dinner between

friends…neighbors!" I stammer, then raise a hopeful eyebrow. "Friendly neighbors?"

"Jason…"

"Kidding. Just kidding, of course…"

"Look, I'll bring Mister Friskies over at 4:30…"

My face screws up. "Who?"

"Mister Friskies."

"Mister…?"

"Friskies!" Megan interrupts. "My cat."

My lips twitch as I try to stifle a laugh. "Your cat's initials are M.F.?"

"So?"

I chuckle softly. "That's pretty hilarious."

She closes her eyes and pinches the bridge of her nose. "You know what? I think I should leave now," she says, clearly reaching the point of exasperation.

"Understood," I say, opening the door. I honestly don't know how I keep screwing up every single conversation I have with every single gorgeous woman I meet. It's like I have a freaking superpower of pure *suck*.

"See you this afternoon," she says as she walks into the hallway before turning around. "Please, just…don't kill my cat, okay?"

"Megan. Come on! It's two days! What could possibly happen?"

o   o   o

She drops off Mister Friskies two hours early, and I hate him from the moment we make eye contact.

9

It's not like he actually does anything to deserve it. I just can't stand animals. They're annoying and territorial, and they constantly pee and poop everywhere they feel the urge. Cats are the worst because they have their stinking litter boxes that you — *the dominant species* — have to clean out all the time. It's insane.

Plus, he just looks weird. All white with black paws and a bizarre black smudge right on his forehead. You'd have thought someone slapped their thumb on an ink pad and wiped it straight up the middle of his head, smudging an ugly streak from eyes to ears. It makes him look ridiculous, but I'm sure Megan finds it endearing.

The things I do for the remote chance of love.

She walks out to the parking lot below and we wave her good-bye, me propping up his paw like some kind of evil puppeteer. There's little question how much we both hate it. As soon as her car is out of sight, I disappear back inside where I grab Mister Friskies by the throat to have a heart-to-heart chat.

"Hey. Dummy. Let's get one thing straight here, shall we? I don't give a *flying fig* about you. Got it? I'm only doing this as a favor for your lady-friend. That is *it*. So stay out of my way, okay?" He tries to squirm away, but I have a decent grip, so he's not going anywhere. His tail is twitching back and forth like a snake preparing to strike, and I hear him let out a low growl.

I reach over with my other hand and start tapping him on his smudge spot. "Uh-uh. No, sir. You give me problems? I'll freakin' give you a bath in the toilet." His eyes actually seem to widen as he stares up at me. "I promise you, if I have to? I *will* make that swirly happen, Mister F. So *knock it off.*" I drop him to the floor and nudge him toward the den with my shoe, making the meanest "don't mess with me" face I can muster. He scampers away and then stops to turn around and scowl at me for a few seconds before slinking off to do Lord knows what.

Two days with this furball? No sweat. I got this.

o   o   o

9:43 p.m., and I'm in the middle of watching Godzilla online when my cell phone rings. I glance at it and frown. It's not Megan calling to check in on her furry friend. It's Mr. Vancil. My boss.

"This is Jason," I answer, realizing how stupid it sounds immediately after. I mean, the guy's calling my cell phone. He knows who it is.

"Ridge? This is Mr. Vancil."

"Oh, hello, sir! How are y—"

"Look," he interrupts, "I don't have much time, so let me get to the point."

"Okay…"

"You've been working on the Mason model the past few weeks? The mansion?"

"Ah… yes, sir! That's correct! It'll be done next Wednesday, just like I promised…"

"I need it tomorrow morning. 7:00 a.m."

Something inside me dies. "Wait, what?" I say, trying hard to mask my panic. *I have five more days! I was supposed to have five more days!!!*

"Mason called. He's going to be in town tomorrow morning. Wants to see what we've come up with. So meet me at the office at..."

"But, you don't want to show him a half-finished model, do you?"

"What? No, of course not!"

"Well, I'm sorry, but there's just no way it'll be done by tomorrow! I mean, I just finished the west wing..." My mouth is starting to fill with cotton even as I feel the rest of my body break into a sweat. "The gazebo alone is gonna take me—"

"The what?"

"The gazebo?" I pause. "Um...the porch-like thing on the outside of—"

"Hell, I *know* what a gazebo is, you moron!" Vancil barks. "I just didn't hear you! Stop mumbling!"

I bite my lip to keep from reacting. "Right. Okay, then. Well, I'm sorry, but you're going to have to call him back and tell him..."

"Excuse me?"

Man, this guy really needs to get his hearing checked. "I SAID," a little louder, "YOU SHOULD CALL MR. MASON AND—"

"Absolutely not! Are you insane? This is our *biggest client*, Ridge! What he wants is what he gets! Period!"

"Okay, but..."

"No buts," he snarls. "Let me make it simple for you: either you come in at 7:00 a.m. tomorrow with that finished Mason model in hand, or you're fired. Clear enough for you?"

That's it? Five faithful years as their top designer and *this* is what it amounts to? A last-minute, Friday-night call with a threat to my job? This is just *wrong*.

"Fine," I say, my eyes narrowing as I watch the gigantic lizard stomping a terrified Tokyo into the ground. "I'll see you in the morning."

He hangs up.

No good-bye, no final chest-beating. Just a cold, quick click.

What a jerk.

o   o   o

I look across the room. The mansion I've been designing is one of the best I've ever done. Ever. It's taken me the better part of a month, working almost non-stop, but it's been worth it. Without question, it's the pinnacle of my career, and arguably the best the firm has ever produced as well. If Mason decides to pass on the project, at least it wouldn't be because of a sucky mock-up, that's for sure.

Can I finish it in the next ten hours? No. There's no way. At least, not finished by my standards. Can cover the crap factor and make it look good enough for a casual observer? Yes. Yes, I can.

"Hey! Friskie-face!" I yell. "Get your furry butt in here!"

Silence.

"Hey! Dorky McDorker! Where you at?" I walk around the apartment searching for him. I can't see him, but there's an odd smell in the air. Something that wasn't there before his arrival. I start to feel sick when I glance at his litter box in the laundry room.

It's empty. But the distinct smell is getting stronger. "Aw, crap."

Now I'm scrambling through the halls to my bedroom, and the unmistakable stench is even thicker. "Crap, crap, crap," I mutter as I step into the room.

"What the...?"

Suddenly I don't care if I ever eat alfredo with Megan again. The only sensation flooding my body at this point is revenge. With a dash of violence.

The first thing to catch my eye is the large, wet circle in the center of my pillow on the bed. My fist tightens beside me as I stand there, frozen. I'm about to launch into a frantic hunt for Mister Friskies when I see movement out of the corner of my eye. Something was moving around in my open closet.

I walk over, pull the door open the rest of the way and look inside. He's right there, back to me and hunched over, lost in concentration as he squeezes a steady stream of steaming cat poo into a neat pile. On my favorite sandal.

He looks over his shoulder at me and lets out a hyper-friendly meow before going back to his work in progress.

"Cat..." I sigh deeply. "I can now honestly say that I really and truly hate your guts."

o   o   o

After locking Sir-Craps-a-Lot in my bathroom and soaking my sandal in a bucket of bleach, I walk back to my office and return to work. He mewls and moans and complains for a good twenty minutes, but I ignore him for the most part. I feel no remorse. It's a universal truth: animals who take dumps on a person's footwear tend to lose privileges. When his whining raises a few octaves, so I slap on a pair of headphones, crank up some choice Morcheeba songs, and get to work.

After working on the model for the next two hours, I've sufficiently impressed myself. The spiral steps are spectacular, the doorways are all in place, and even the miniature windows are looking good. I smile, satisfaction spreading throughout my body. *You know,* I think to myself, *I might just survive this crazy night after all.*

I grab the X-Acto knife and start working on the gazebo. It isn't going to be as difficult as I thought, but it's clearly going to take some considerable carving time to make the pieces fit the way I want them to. As I begin to cut into the wood, however, there's suddenly a loud *thump* above me.

I jump, managing to not only nick the gazebo, but somehow stabbing myself in the finger to boot. I curse loudly, jumping back from the table, the blade falling to the floor where it embeds itself into the carpet, pointy side down. I squeeze my finger as I glare at the ceiling. *How in the* hell *did that cat get up there?*

"Hate you, hate you, HATE YOU CAT!" I mutter as I run down the hall to the bathroom. I thrust open the door, jam my finger under the faucet, and turn on the cold water. It stings for a few seconds, but soon the blood slows and the pain begins to dull. I grab a handful of toilet paper, press down hard against the wound, and that's when I see him.

Mister Friskies is sprawled out across my bathmat, not moving. I can't even tell if he's breathing. I throw my wad of toilet paper at him, hitting him in the gut. He groggily lifts his head to see what I'm doing, then stretches and yawns before closing his eyes and returning to his comfy coma.

Stupid cat.

I think about spraying him with water when a thought slowly begins to percolate in my mind. *Wait a second…if he's in here, then what was…*

Something scurries across the ceiling panels above me, running back toward the office. I stare at the ceiling, then down at the cat. Then back at the ceiling.

What is *that? A rat? No, that sounds too big to be a rat. A raccoon, maybe? Or a possum? Man, I hope not. Those things are just plain nasty.*

Then I have an idea. A brilliant idea. A super-sparkly happy thought.

"Hey. Snooze-a-Lot."

The cat ignores me.

"Wanna have some fun?"

o   o   o

It takes me a few minutes before I find the access panel, but eventually I locate it in the laundry room along with my long-lost step stool. I consider opening it up, sticking my head in quickly and shining the flashlight around to get a good look.

16

Then I remember the gazebo. *Forget it. Just stick the cat up there and get back to work.*

I open the panel, grab the cat off the washing machine, and thrust him up into the blackness of the attic.

"There. You're free to roam. Go make a new friend or something..." I shut the panel behind him. Then I frown at the thought. "Hey. On second thought? If that's one of your lady-friends up there? Just leave her alone. I really don't wanna hear you two going at it. Got it?"

Silence. Then the fading pitter patter of little feet as he starts to explore.

I smile. "Nice kitty..."

o   o   o

Over the next thirty minutes I completely forget about Mister Friskies, I'm so engrossed in finishing the project. The gazebo's complete except for the steps leading up to it, but those will only take a few minutes. For the most part? I think I'm done. Done! And it looks fantastic. Better than I had ever hoped.

I back away from the table, fold my arms across my chest, and admire my work. It really is breathtaking, my attention to detail. Mr. Vancil is going to regret threatening my job, that's for sure. After creating this masterpiece, I'll be able to work at any design firm in the city. No question. All I need are some professional, high resolution photos to stick in my portfolio.

I retrieve my camera and tripod from the closet, setting it up so my first few photos will effectively showcase the whole thing. I'm looking through the viewfinder to adjust the light balance when I hear it.

The first set of muted thumps makes me smile. "'Atta boy, Friskies. Give him what for." But then there's a loud, low growl followed by sudden scuffling from the middle of the ceiling toward the wall.

"Hey. Everything alright up there?"

The growling grows louder, and I watch in horror as the ceiling tile above the desk shakes for a moment, then starts to buckle. Something inside me shrivels up.

Oh, no... no, no, no, no, NO!!!

I run toward the desk, but I already know I'm too late. A split-second later the ceiling tile collapses under the weight, and Mister Friskies craters into the dead center of the model, along with something...else...on top of him. While it's the same size as Friskies, it's not a raccoon or a possum. Or even a cat, for that matter. In fact, it's not like anything I've ever seen before in my life.

The creature is all black and covered in what looks like wet, reptilian scales. It holds the cat firmly in its claws, with a thin tail wrapped tightly around his midsection and a stinger that appears to be piercing him in the throat. Mister Friskies thrashes about madly, desperately trying to escape as the creature continues to stab it with its stinger. The two of them roll across the entire desk, crushing what's left of my life's best work. My masterpiece. Created in weeks, destroyed in seconds.

Ignoring the commotion, I quietly pick up my X-Acto knife off the floor. I don't know what that thing is. I have no freaking clue what sort of twisted, demonic gecko is trying to deflate Mister Friskies with his stinger while destroying what was left of my once promising career.

But I do know this: I'm going to stab that thing in the head until it looks like moldy Swiss cheese. And when it's dead? I'm going to find its eyes and stab the sockets until I stop sobbing. And then, when I'm done with that...thing... when I feel I've fully avenged myself by killing it and sending it back to whatever hell it came from...

If he hasn't died at that point? Then I swear...

...I'm going to kill that cat.

Author's Note

Here's the thing about cats: I LOVE cats.

I actually consider them one of the more intelligent varieties of pets. When Kim and I were first married, we bought a cat. A yellow-eyed, classic black cat named Yahtzee. A year later, we bought her a playmate, a calico kitten named Pixie. Yahtzee hated Pixie with a passion, but we loved 'em both.

The summer I wrote "Model Pet," we were watching a friend's cat, Ninja. Around that time we also had an issue with some kind of noisy thing up in our attic, prancing about on our ceiling tiles at all hours of the day (or night). So as my mind wandered one night, I envisioned what it would be like if a character stuck a cat into the ceiling and the thing it found wasn't a rat at all.

Two days later, and "Model Pet" was born.

ASSASSIN'S SUICIDE

"See you tomorrow, Alice." Joseph Cho walked past his secretary's desk, stopping briefly outside his office to remove his coat from the hanger. It had been an extremely strenuous Monday at Shield Bank and Trust, working out the final details in the Montola merger. Joseph sighed. He was ready to go home, relax with a few laps in the pool, and go to bed by nine.

Alice looked up from her computer. "Have a good night, Mr. Cho," she said. "Hope tomorrow's as much fun as today was," she said with a smirk.

"Oh Lord," he sighed with a smile, "I don't believe my body can take much more fun." He gave her a casual wink and slipped through the glass doors into the hallway.

Alice was a one of a kind worker — the kind who was constantly dependable, forever loyal, and yet possessed enough personality to keep a guy on his feet. In all honesty, Joseph had to admit that he expected a loafer ten years ago when he decided to hire through a temporary agency. He had been pleasantly surprised to find a diamond like Alice had slipped through the prospective cracks. Because of Shield Bank and Trust's recent expansion outside of Las Vegas, he was glad to finally be able to give indispensable workers like Alice the well-earned bonuses they deserved.

He walked down the hall to the elevators and pressed a button on his key ring, calling his private elevator into action. Originally the idea of having his own executive elevator was one he disliked intensely, yet the head office in Seoul had insisted on it. *To ensure the utmost in safety and security*, the memo had read, *we provide all Shield Bank and Trust executives with private elevators.* While Joseph still considered it was an unnecessary waste of time and money for the most part, he did have to admit that after the day he had, the idea of getting into his own elevator did hold a certain appeal.

A faint chime sounded above him, announcing the elevator's arrival, and Joseph picked up his briefcase and stepped onto the plush carpet. He turned around to push the down button and was shocked to see a man leaning against the corner, arms folded casually across his chest.

"What the...? How did you get in here?" Joseph demanded, backing away.

"Shut up, old man."

Joseph darted toward the open doors. The man's arm shot out in front of him, shoving him backwards into the back wall. "I don't think so," he said. He reached down and pushed the Close Door button, continuing to stare at him with cold, unwavering eyes.

"Do I know you?" Joseph asked, scrutinizing the man's face.

"Nah."

"Well, then may I ask what is this all about? Do you want money? Is that it?" He set his briefcase down and began to reach into his coat. "Let's not do that, shall we?" The man reached over and grabbed Joseph's arm by the sleeves, pulling it back. He let go and motioned for him to move into the opposite corner. Joseph looked at him, perplexed, but did as he was instructed.

"My name's Dex. I'm here on behalf of the Montola family. Seems they're having a problem communicating with you. Guess you could call me their 'communications consultant.'"

"What problem?" Joseph asked, frowning. "Everything is progressing perfectly from what I understand. The merger is in its final draft stages. In another week it will be finished. Cho-Montola Enterprises will be complete."

"Y'see, *that's* the problem I'm talkin' about," Dex said. "Thing is, Manny Montola don't really *wanna* merge with you guys. You chinks came in here and found a loophole in the system, thinkin' you can just take over our country, one business at a time?" His breath became short and strained, his voice rising in volume. "Well, ya *can't*! Y'see, there're guys back in Chicago, guys who don't want to see Montola merged. Guys who called me up last night to make sure it don't."

Joseph couldn't hide the smirk forming on his face. "So…you're here to do…what? Talk me out of it? Break my fingers, perhaps? My arms or legs? Or wait, let me guess…" He looked directly into Dex's cold eyes. "You're here to *assassinate* me?"

Dex's face flushed. "You think death is something to joke about, old man?" he said, leaning forward a few inches.

The smile faded from Joseph's face. "Oh, no. No, I

do not. There's nothing funny about death at all. It's just...well..." He paused to stifle a chuckle. "Where's your gun?"

"Don't need one."

"Knife?"

"Nope."

"Poisonous dart?"

"Please."

"What, you're just going to kill me with your bare hands?"

"Not exactly."

Mr. Cho stared at him for a few more seconds, trying to get a read on his opponent's face. Finally he shrugged. "I give up," he sighed.

Dex looked down at his feet, drawing in a deep breath and exhaling it slowly. "Tell the truth, I never told anyone *how* I do what I do. But seein' as how you'll be dead in a few minutes, I guess you can be the first."

"I feel so very privileged," Joseph murmured.

"Shut up an' listen." Dex paused to collect his thoughts. "So, I got this...gift, y'see? It's kinda like what the scientists call 'telekinesis,' but I can't exactly move things across a table to bend spoons or nothin'. I just...well...I create chaos."

"Chaos?"

"I like to call it the 'Chaos Touch,' 'cause whatever I focus on gets screwed up. When I first discovered it as a kid, I used to break the bras of all the girls. All I'd do is look at 'em and concentrate, an' the next thing you know? Snap!" He giggled to himself. "Anyhow, later on I figured out how to focus it, to kinda aim it an' stuff. Didn't take me too long before

I figured out I could make some serious money by my being a freak."

Joseph nodded his head and chuckled. "I'm impressed. Montola sends a telekinetic assassin to 'take care of me.' May I ask how many people you have killed with this...ah... 'Chaos Touch?'"

Dex shrugged. "Aw, I dunno. Fifty? Mebbe seventy-five? I stopped counting a long time ago."

"Why you?"

"Why me?"

"Yes," Joseph continued. "Why, exactly, would they send *you* to kill *me*?"

Dex snorted. "'Cause I asked 'em to."

Joseph's eyebrows raised in surprise. "Is that so?"

"Yeah, it is. This one's personal."

"But...I thought you said you didn't know me..."

"I don't. But I knew Tony and Tommy, an' you killed 'em. Last week."

Joseph frowned. His eyes floated around the confines of the elevator, searching his memory. "No...I don't believe I killed anyone recently. Are you sure you don't have me confused for another gentlemen. We do all look alike, after all." He looked over at Dex and smiled.

Dex continued to glare at him. "Tony and Tommy came for you, but your boys somehow spotted them before they popped ya."

"Excuse me, but did you say 'your boys?'"

"Yeah."

"I'm afraid I don't have any 'boys.'"

"Boys. Bodyguards. Whatever you wanna call 'em..."

Joseph shook his head. "I'm sorry, but I don't

employ any bodyguards."

"Just cut it out, okay! They both had their brains blown out, okay? Now, granted," he paused, holding a hand up. "Turns out Max's gun backfired on him, blowing his ugly mug out the back of his head. But even at that, those guys were friends of mine." A fury burned in his eyes as he stared at him, shaking his head in disgust. "Good friends. So when I heard they needed someone who never botched a job yet, I said I'd do it."

"I'm sorry. You've never once failed?"

"Nope."

"Not once?"

"That would be what 'nope' means, right?"

"Well, now I'm impressed," Joseph said, smiling. Dex took his hand out of his pocket. Joseph looked down and saw it was empty. He watched as the assassin extended his index finger and thumb, forming them into the crude shape of a gun.

"You know," Joseph said, shrugging. "I could use someone like you. Someone with your...*unique*...skill set."

"Forget it. This ain't for the money no more. It's for Tommy an' Tony! They didn't deserve to go like that, man!"

Joseph looked down at the finger pointed at his head. "I understand your anger, but I sincerely wish you would reconsider. For your sake."

"For *my* sake?" Dex laughed. "What the hell are you talking about? It's just you an' me, old man. Ain't nobody saving you this time!"

"Please..."

"Just shut up, okay? I'm tired of wastin' time here.

I wanna go to bed early tonight, y'know?" He stretched his arm out and pointed directly at Joseph's heart.

"Bang."

The word was uttered in a normal voice, but the silence that followed made it sound like it had been shouted. Both men stood there, unmoving, staring at each other in the stillness of the crowded corridor.

An instant later, a look of surprise shot into Dex's eyes, followed by the unmistakable expression of pain. He reached up with his hand, clutching at his chest.

"You really should have let me explain myself," Joseph began, reaching past Dex and pushing the down button. "You see, I, too, have a special kind of 'gift.' I call it the 'Refraction Factor,' for lack of a better term. Ever since I was a young child, I came to realize that I could never be harmed by another person." He paused and moved aside as Dex sank to his knees, wheezing as his breath became increasingly labored and strained.

"In fact," Joseph continued, "I soon discovered that if anyone even *tried* to hurt me, their efforts were actually reflected back upon *them*. Poisons, knifes, guns—nothing works. *Ever*. Which is why I'm so successful at what I do. Everyone the bank sent before me kept dying, *especially* when they tried to acquire the Montola property. Unfortunately, that commodity is far too valuable to pass up, so they called me in to finalize everything."

He looked down and smiled at Dex's whitening face, contorted with pain. He watched as a thin stream of blood began to trickle down from his nose.

"I'd say everything is pretty final, now. Wouldn't you?"

The elevator doors opened and Joseph stepped through the doors and turned around. "It was a pleasure to meet you, Dex. I do wish things had turned out differently." He turned and walked toward his car, relishing the chilled briskness of the parking garage. "And please," he called out behind him, "Do try to bleed into your hands, won't you? I just had the carpet cleaned."

Jack Kardiac

A LIGHT SNACK

It doesn't remember the last time it ate. Its miniature brain can't conjure up the image of the creature it sprang upon last, how it ripped its belly open with its powerful muzzle, rending it to shreds with each savage bite. Memories of yesterday fade from its consciousness like the surrounding jungle mist evaporating with the rising sun. Oblivious of the past, the creature is conscious of only the present, moment by moment. One alarming sensation continues to override the others with its persistence.

Hunger. It hungers again.

The moist air melts with the sun's rekindled glare, dousing the trees with a soft, sticky mist. Roused by its gnawing emptiness, the reptile stands upright on its strong, oversized legs, muscles quivering as they stretch, straining to shake off the night's slumber and restore their full functionality once more. Off to its right a flock of pterodactyls quickly takes flight, seemingly sensing its approach. Swiftly cocking a head to one side, it watches the flock with a wide eye, straining to get a better look at the possible prey.

A stream of saliva escapes its slackened jaws, the tiny rivulet trickling onto its coarse, leathery chest. As the winged creatures fade into the yellowing sky, they subsequently dissolve from the predator's fuzzy focus. With its undersized arms flailing awkwardly against its oversized body, the dinosaur tramples the vegetation below it as it begins the renewed search for sustenance.

Bounding across the thick jungle loam, it carelessly plods through the thick brush to flush out some form of breakfast. Within minutes it comes upon a family of smaller creatures — undoubtedly close cousins of some sort — as they frantically scurry away to avoid the beast's fatal attention. The prospect of dinner clearly in sight, the hunter bounds forward in eager pursuit of the miniature pack. Emitting a flurry of high-pitched shrieks and peeps, the smaller reptiles scamper beneath fallen trees and inside stray burrows in the soft soil, desperately trying to escape.

Despite its erratic darting between trees and shrubs, one of the slower creatures lags behind in its confusion and is quickly pinned beneath the crushing foot of its pursuant. It releases a final, frantic shriek before its head is detached with a single, voracious bite of the larger creature's giant jaws.

Lodging its sharp rows of teeth deeper into its prey, the carnivore jerks back violently, tearing open the stomach with a sudden splattering of rich, crimson blood. Intestines spill lazily down its side, forming a sloppy pile on the ground beside it.

The beast doesn't stop to catch a breath, chewing and ripping and rending the soft sinews below, each swallow providing it with minimal satisfaction, only serving to further escalate its eternal bloodlust. Still standing on its prey, the carnivore raises its head to bolt down the fresh meat, stopping for a few seconds to survey the surrounding area. Finding no challengers or possible threats to its new meal, it lowers its head and tears off another chunk out of the light yellow belly, the jungle floor now soaked with the blood flowing freely from the creature's carcass.

After consuming half of its light snack, the dinosaur releases a roar of triumph to the jungle it owns. It's flooded with emotion, a combination of peace, power, and invincibility. It has once again conquered a lesser creature, reasserting itself as the jungle's rightful ruler. There are no worthy competitors — nothing in the jungle can harm it — nothing would dare to try, lest it face a grim death at the jaws of nature's selected royalty.

Its attention diverts from its organic chew toy as it spots the slender neck of a brachiosaurus rising above a growth of trees a short distance away. The snack was satisfying, but the beast's appetite for fresh flesh remains far from satiated. It doesn't consider the larger dinosaur's size in comparison with its own; instead its mind obsesses with the image of pouncing upon the clueless creature. It envisions digging knifelike jaws deep into its side and drinking in the coppery blood as it slices through the slender, tender neck. Abandoning the half-eaten carcass to spoil in the sun, the creature quickly advances through the brush in pursuit of its latest lunch.

The brachiosaurus doesn't notice the creature that now hunts it, consumed with bloodlust. Instead, it casually lowers its head once again to graze on the lush jungle growth flourishing around it. Oblivious of any possible danger, it sluggishly turns away from the approaching predator to chew the succulent leaves of an adjacent tree, lazily surveying the lush marshland surrounding it.

The distance between them diminishes with every step of the predator's feverish sprint, its minute brain crazed as it anticipates the satisfaction of the kill. Within seconds it will leap upon the great beast's back, slicing open its thick tissues with its powerful jaws to be violently devoured with relentless urgency. It spots an opening in the thick foliage ahead of it, and its pace quickens.

Suddenly the creature is enveloped with the blackness of a gigantic shadow from above. Before it can react to the anomaly, it is instantly pinned by the crushing foot of the Tyrannosaurus rex. Trapped beneath the awesome weight of the larger hunter, the Velociraptor releases a final, frantic shriek before its head is detached with a single, voracious bite of the T. rex's giant jaws.

Lodging its sharp rows of teeth deeper into its prey, the Tyrannosaurus jerks back violently, tearing the body wide open with a sudden splattering of rich, crimson blood.

Standing on the remains of its prey, the Tyrannosaurus raises its head and bolts down its meat, returning to tear off another chunk out of the light yellow belly, the jungle floor now soaked with the blood flowing freely from the creature's carcass.

As it consumes its light snack, the T. rex releases a roar of triumph to alert the surrounding jungle that it is once again the rightful ruler.

SNAPDRAGON

"I said I wanted *pink* ponies!"

Ju's mother stared at her daughter in disbelief. After spending the past four months and tens of thousands of dollars on the girl's eighth birthday, meticulously planning every minute detail, her daughter still had the gall to throw a tantrum. On the morning of the party, no less. Jin-Kim closed her eyes, inhaling deeply, praying for serenity and patience.

"Darling, I understand that you want pink ponies," she said soothingly. "However, the County Animal Control Department strictly forbids the coloring of animals for entertainment purposes…"

"They did it in Wizard of Oz."

Jin-Kim opened her eyes. "Excuse me?"

Ju's frown sank deeper. "In the movie. *The Wizard of Oz*! They had green ponies in it."

"Okay, well…"

"So if they did it back then for the movie, why can't you do it for me now?" She stood by the doorway and put her hands on her hips. "I *want* pink ponies, *Mother*! And I want them *now. Today.*"

"Yes. Well, I'm sorry, honey, but your party begins in a few hours and there's simply no way we can possibly—"

"You and Daddy don't love me."

Ju bolted out the door and ran down the stairs,

trying her hardest to make it sound like she was genuinely crying. In truth, she couldn't care less about the color of the ponies. It wasn't about the ponies. It was about control, and she had learned from her father years ago that the best way to control other people was by manipulating their emotions. And out of the virtual deck of emotions to play with, expressing extreme disappointment in her parents had always been Ju's trump card.

Jin-Kim stood speechless, staring at the doorway where her daughter had stood. She knew she should feel some kind of pain at the biting words, but the scene was so familiar to her that the only emotion she felt now was a welcome wave of relief the conversation was over. After years of spontaneous tantrums, verbal manipulation, and more emotional outbursts than she cared to recall, she'd simply grown tired of arguing with Ju. It wasn't worth her time and energy anymore.

She crossed the expansive bedroom to the bar and was about to pour herself a drink when the doorbell rang down on the first floor. She frowned, reviewing the mental checklists in her head.

Pony rustlers…Cirque du Soleil performers…the pedicure and manicure team…

No, they were all in place and ready, and she wasn't expecting any guests until 4:30 p.m., at the earliest. She frowned, placing her glass and bottle down on the counter.

"Lucy?" she called out. "Lucy, if you're still downstairs could you be a dear and get the door, please?"

From beyond the hall a faint voice echoed from

the kitchen. "Yes, Mrs. Jin. Right away."

Jin-Kim smiled. Lucy was by far one of the best helpers they had hired since moving to Las Vegas. Reliable, professional, and friendly, she was easily worth her wages, if not twice as much.

A few minutes and two quick drinks later, there was a gentle knock on the doorframe. Jin-Kim looked up from the empty glass she'd been staring at in her hand, her reverie broken by the interruption.

"Yes? Who is it?"

Lucy meekly peeked around the corner, avoiding eye contact. "Sorry to disturb, Mrs. Jin. But you have a visitor downstairs and…"

"Alright. Thank you, I'll be right down," Jin-Kim sighed, rubbing the bridge of her nose.

Lucy looked frightened. "Ma'am…I'm sorry, but…"

"I'm not getting any younger," a shrill voice called from the stairwell.

Jin-Kim froze. She knew that voice. That *tone*. She would recognize it anywhere. She pinched the bridge of her nose and closed her eyes, sighing as she shook her head in disbelief.

Mother.

o   o   o

"Mother, what are you doing here?"

Jin-Kim poured a glass of water for her mother as they stood across from each other in the kitchen. "I mean, we weren't expecting you until *next* week."

"Oh, I know," the older woman gushed, waving her hand dismissively. "But when I thought about how silly it was, my missing Ju's birthday by only a week. Well, that just seemed like poor planning on my part, don't you think?" She sat down at the table and started to sip on the water.

Jin-Kim stared at her, not answering. She was still wrapping her head around the fact that her mother was sitting there, in her kitchen, crashing her daughter's birthday party on purpose. She had long been accustomed to being controlled as a child, but discovered that even as an adult she was still trying to break free of her mother's subtle manipulations, with little success.

"I suppose it was," she said quietly as she sat down across the table from her. She forced a smile, glad that Lucy hadn't shown her mother upstairs. Being scolded for relaxing with a few drinks before the party was the *last* thing she needed today.

"So," her mother asked, flashing an exuberant grin. "Where is my little princess?"

Jin-Kim waved her hand around nonchalantly. "Oh, I'm sure she's around here somewhere…"

"Well, I can't *wait* to see her. She's going to be so *excited*!" She stifled a girlish giggle and stood up to search the house for her angel.

"Why?" Jin-Kim asked.

Her mother turned around. "Why what, dear?"

"Why is Ju going to be so excited, exactly?"

"Why, because of her gift, of course!"

Jin-Kim watched her walk away, glad to part company until she spied the bright red box her mother was carrying with her. It was short, thick, and had three evenly-spaced air holes on the side. Her eyes widened in alarm.

"Mother!" she snapped, standing to her feet.

Her mother stopped in the doorway, turning around slowly. "Yes?" she asked innocently.

"What are you doing, Mother." It was an accusation, not a question. She glared at the box tucked under her arm.

Her mother paused, trying hard to conjure up the most clueless appearance she could. "Why, whatever do you mean?"

"The *box,* Mother."

A pause. "Yes?"

"Please tell me that's not what I think it is."

Her mother's smile vanished. "Well, it's not a puppy, if that's what you're afraid of."

"I *know* it's not a puppy, Mother."

"Well, if you know it's not a puppy, then why did you—"

Jin-Kim held up a hand, exasperated. "Mother. Please. Just…stop."

Her mother walked back over to her, gently placing the box down on the kitchen counter. "Jin-Kim…"

"She's not ready."

A silence hung in the air as the two women stared each other down. The older woman's gaze fixed with a knowing glare while her daughter tried to muster the sternest, most stubborn look she could imagine.

"She is," her mother nodded slowly, smiling at her.

"No. She's not."

"Yes, Jin-Kim," her mother insisted again. "*She is.* Trust me."

Jin-Kim rolled her eyes. "Mother, please. You do realize she's—"

"What I know," her mother interrupted angrily, "is that Ju is in constant danger living here in this city. In this *country*." She paused for effect. "She's in danger of losing her heritage, of losing what makes her special. Of losing what—"

"She's an *American*, Mother. You can't change that."

"Yes, I know she's American," her mother conceded. "But she's also Korean, and I won't allow her to be raised here unprepared. Un*protected*."

"Ju *is* protected! We've taken every precaution, we even—"

"Jin-Kim!"

Her mother glared at her, eyes ablaze, fighting to control the emotions bubbling up inside her. A quick burst of crimson flushed across her face before it resumed its normal hue, her breathing slowly subsiding. "That is enough. This is a family *tradition*! A rare gift! An *honor*! She *is* ready. I know it, and you know it."

Jin-Kim looked away and shook her head angrily. Even at thirty-two, her mother still had the uncanny ability to make her feel like a child again. Unheard. Unappreciated. Unloved. She almost shivered as she felt a fresh layer of bitter resentment pour over her heart.

Finally she shrugged her shoulders in defeat. "Whatever," she sighed. "But she's not going to like it, you realize. She's a pink princess who dreams of ponies and unicorns and sugar and spice and everything nice. So just be prepared."

"She will love it," her mother insisted. "You will see."

o   o   o

Four hours later after the private concert, advance movie screening, and pony rides, Ju and all her friends gathered around in the backyard pavilion where she began to unwrap her presents.

When she was done, her grandmother quietly approached her from the side, whispered in her ear, and presented her with the small, red box. The kids all crowded around her, squealing with delight at the final present, but Ju's grandmother shooed them away, kindly asking them to keep their distance and quiet down so they wouldn't disturb such a sacred moment.

Ju glanced around the large room until she was absolutely sure she was the center of everyone's attention, caught her mother's look of disapproval, and then unhitched the box's clasp, lifted the lid, and peered inside. She gasped, her face frozen in a mixture of confusion and trepidation. She glanced up at her grandmother, her eyebrows knit with concern.

Her grandmother smiled, nodding her head. "It's okay," she whispered. "You are ready, Ju."

She looked back in the box, then up at her grandmother again. Her face broke out in a wide grin. She removed the lid entirely and calmly reached inside, removing the creature from within. She held it up high for the room to see, beaming with pride.

The crowd of children all backed away, terrified at the animal that now stared back at them with cold, unblinking eyes. A small, pink tongue darted out and back into its mouth, causing a handful of girls to shriek loudly and run back into the house to escape.

Ju looked back over at her grandmother and smiled. "Thank you," she mouthed silently. Her grandmother nodded in knowing reassurance, beaming inside as she found her daughter's frustrated glare in the crowd of impressed guests.

"He has no name yet, Ju," she said, leaning closer to Ju. "What would you like to name him?"

Ju turned the creature around in her hands, cocked her head as she looked deep into its eyes, and lost herself in thought for a few seconds.

She smiled, eyes suddenly alight with excitement.

"Snapdragon," she said with pride. "His name is Snapdragon."

o　　o　　o

"Stupid Mrs. Stamper," Ju muttered to herself as she walked down the sidewalk, her bright pink Hello Kitty backpack slung over her shoulder. "Can't believe she yelled at me in front of *everyone*. How was *I* supposed to know I couldn't bring you to school? Bethany brought *her* butt-ugly mouse last week! And it's not like you'd ever actually hurt anyone." She balled her fists as she walked, the scowl on her face growing more severe with every step.

"Hate her. I hate them *all!*"

She lashed out with her foot on the sidewalk, inadvertently kicking a pinecone down the sidewalk ahead of her. She watched as it bounced crazily down the path until it came to rest next to a pair of sandals. The feet inside were covered with a pair of stark white socks.

Ju stopped walking and looked up, staring in shock at the man standing in the middle of the sidewalk. He wore a bright orange Hawaiian shirt, knee-length shorts, and had an overstuffed blue fanny pack strapped around his waist.

He looked utterly ridiculous. Ju didn't laugh.

She glanced at the blue van behind him, immediately noticing it was parked far closer to the curb than necessary, and even from her distance she could see the sliding side door was slightly ajar. The hairs on her arm stood up, and she swallowed nervously, carefully retaining eye contact.

"S'okay," the man said, bending down to pick up the pinecone. "I got it." He flashed her a fake smile, extending his hand out toward her. "Here ya go."

She didn't speak, but continued to glare at him, unflinching.

The man raised his eyebrows. "No? Well, okay then…" He shrugged his shoulders, tossing the pinecone beside the tree. He continued to stand in the middle of the sidewalk, put his hands in his pockets and pretended to stare with great interest at the tree between them. After a few seconds he jutted his chin out, nodding toward the trunk. "Big tree, isn't it?" he asked.

Ju studied his attire and squinted to block out some of the harsh glare of his shirt. "Do I know you from somewhere?"

"Nah," the man said, shaking his head. "I don't think so."

She rolled her eyes at him and sighed. "What do you want?" she said bluntly.

He flashed a look of mock surprise at her. "What do you mean? I'm just…"

"What. The crap. Do you want."

His smile vanished. "Well, now. You get right to the point, don't you Missy?"

"You do know who I am, right? Who my *father* is?"

"Who your father…" he chuckled, shaking his head. "Let's just say that we wouldn't be here if we didn't."

"Then you also know that I'm not alone, and you're about to get your butts shot to pot," she said, smiling.

The man smiled. "Is that so? What? You mean…by *those* guys?" he pointed over her shoulder. She glanced over at the black SUV parked twenty yards behind her, gasped when she saw the blood-stained windshield.

"Yeeeaah," the man continued, "They've been effectively…what's the word…? *Neutralized*."

She looked back at him, her eyes boring her fury into him.

"Sorry to rain on your parade, girlie." He pulled out his other hand and held up a small black box. A blue arc shot across it for a split second, the air between them crackling loudly. "Now, let's not make a fuss, shall we? Just get in the van and nobody'll get hurt."

Ju didn't move. "I can run."

"I can run faster."

She studied him for a few seconds, silently

43

calculating probabilities in her head. A second later she looked around the street, carefully weighing her other options.

"Seriously, kid. I hear these things will make you poop yourself when you get zapped. And I'd rather not change your diaper if I don't have to, you know?" He frowned. "Listen closely. If you run, I *will* catch you. And when I do, I *will tase* you. And you *will* poop your panties. I promise."

"Tase isn't a verb."

"Excuse me?"

"Taser is a proper noun. Based on the acronym T.A.S.E.R., for Thomas A. Swift's Electric Rifle."

The man released another hair-raising crackle of energy into the air. "Do I look like I care?"

Ju sighed, shaking her head in disgust. "Fine," she said, walking over to him. "But you *do* realize this will not end well for you, don't you? Because when…"

"Come *on* already! Save the speech and just get in the freakin' van…" He opened the side door and shoved her in, holding the taser between them.

"What, you ladies having a little social chat out there? What the hell took so long?" a second man in the front seat demanded. He glanced nervously from the man to Ju and back out the front windshield, pulling away from the curb.

"Kid's a chatterbox. Thought she was gonna outsmart me or something."

"Oh yeah?" the driver sneered into the rearview mirror. "Well, you *ain't*, girlie girl! We're what you call 'professionals,' see? So if you ever wanna see your mommy or daddy again, you're gonna do exactly what we say. Got that?" He looked around the neighborhood nervously and shifted the van into gear, pulling away from the curb.

"Professionals, huh?" Ju asked.

"That's right," he continued. "S'why we wore these stupid shirts." He held up his arm so she could admire the floral print of his blue shirt, equally as obnoxious as his partner's. "We're just your average, everyday Vegas tourists. Nothin' to see here, move along people, move along..."

His friend snickered, then padded his fanny pack. "But I gotta admit, this thing does come in handy." He grinned at her. "You know, sticking all your stuff in your pockets just gets old. But this puppy can hold it all. Taser, cell phone, my pocket knife, even..."

"Crap!" the driver yelled. "Crap! *Crap!*" He glanced into the rearview mirror, then back at the road.

"What?!"

"Her cell phone! Grab her cell phone!"

His eyes widened, but just before he lunged across the van to search for it, Ju reached into her pocket and pulled it out, holding it out to him.

"Here," she said, fighting the urge to laugh.

He snatched it out of her hand, confused. "Thanks..." he said, glancing down at it.

"Tanner!"

"What? Stop yelling at me!"

"The phone!"

"I know! I got it! Relax already!"

"No, you idiot! You gotta take the battery out! Otherwise, they can track her using GPS or something!"

Tanner looked down at the phone, then at the taser, and back over to Ju. He carefully placed the taser between his knees, still pointing it in her direction. "Don't try anything stupid," he growled.

Ju stared at him. "Don't worry about it," she said, smirking at him. "Tanner."

He frowned. "Dammit. Steve, she knows our names!"

"You...! I can't believe you just...!" Steve blubbered, still managing to change lanes. "You are such a MORON!"

"What? What'd I do?"

"She didn't know *my* name until you said it just now, doofus!"

Tanner looked back at Ju, his shoulders slumping. "Aw, man...."

Steve punched the steering wheel, letting out a string of expletives. He shook his head in disbelief. "You are so...so..."

"Look, I'm sorry, okay? I'm sorry, I'm sorry, I'M SORRY! Jeez!"

"TANNER! Shut up and focus! Take the battery out of the phone already!" He turned on his signal and merged into the freeway traffic.

Tanner fumbled with the phone, dropping the taser on the floor. He glared at Ju, making sure she didn't move, then retrieved it and wedged it between his sandals. He ripped the back of the cell phone off, grabbed the battery and flung it over Ju's head toward the back of the van. It slammed into one of the back windows, cracking it with a spectacular spider web.

"Tanner! What..."

"I got it!" Tanner interrupted. "Okay? I got the battery. The phone's dead now. Alright? It's dead."

Steve shot him a look in the mirror, then shook his head again. "Amateur…" he muttered to himself.

Tanner opened his mouth to say something, but thought better of it. He turned back to stare at Ju, who was still smirking at him. He glared at her. "What?" he demanded.

"I didn't say anything."

"You think that was funny?"

"Not at all," Ju said, trying to hide her delight at his ineptitude. She looked out the front window, folding her hands in her lap.

"Put your stupid seatbelt on," he snarled at her.

Ju sighed, then reached over and pulled the belt across her, snapping it into place. "Happy?" she asked.

He stared at her for a few seconds, glanced up at the broken window again and shook his head in shame. His eyes wandered down to her backpack, and he shifted in his seat, scowling.

"What's in the book bag?" he asked.

Ju's body tensed for a second, then relaxed. She stared at the floor, avoiding eye contact with him. "Books," she said, shrugging.

He leaned closer, trying his best to look as menacing as he could. "What else?"

She leaned forward an inch, staring back at him. "More books." Then she sat back smugly. "And a pink protractor."

"You'd better check her backpack, too," Steve said from the front seat. "They might've stuck some kinda GPS location tracker thing in there."

"I know, I'm doing it, man..."

"Check for a hidden pocket in the liner or something, or..."

Tanner's neck whipped around fast. "I said I *got* this! So shut up already!"

"Just do it, Tanner! Stop screwing around!"

Tanner turned back toward Ju. He held his hand out. "Gimme the bag," he said.

Ju shook her head no.

He leaned in closer, wagging the taser between two fingers. "Really? You don't remember this? My friend Mr. Pants Pooper?" She stared at him, visibly frightened. "Give. Me. The bag," he said coldly.

She shook her head again, clutching the backpack tighter.

"Well," he said, shaking his head in disappointment. "Can't say I didn't try..." Before she could react, he leapt across the van, slapped her across the face and yanked the backpack out of her hands.

Ju gasped. In her entire eight years of life, she had never been violently touched like that. No spankings, no hand slaps, no physical attacks of any kind. Until today.

The unwanted tears started to flood her eyes, her hand instinctively rising to touch her cheek to soothe the burning sensation that now spread across it.

She opened her eyes enough to see Tanner had flung the bag between his feet, and was actually smiling at her. Ju's eyes narrowed as she glared at him.

"You will pay dearly for that," she threatened through clenched teeth.

"Oh really? Yeah, I don't think so. In fact, I think it's *you* who's gonna pay dearly. Or your parents will, at least..." He chuckled at his own joke, then reached down and unzipped the bag. "And just for the record? It didn't have to go down like that. It was your stupid decision, you know."

"You are the stupid one," she hissed.

"Sticks and stones, girlie."

He stuck out his tongue and thrust in his hand into the book bag.

Ju smiled.

Tanner screamed. "What the...! Ow! Ahhhhhh...!"

A look of pain and confusion flashed into his eyes, and he yanked his hand out of the back, along with the lizard now firmly attached to it. "Ah! Get if off! Get it off!"

He flailed his hand from side to side, frantically trying to shake it off. It not only held on tight, but latched on even tighter, its razor-sharp teeth slicing a wider slash across his hand with every shake.

Tanner wrapped his other hand around its neck and tried to pull it off. The sharp, serrated teeth dug even deeper, cutting into bone. He screamed again.

"What the hell are you doing back there?" Steve yelled from the front seat, trying to drive while simultaneously glancing in the rearview mirror.

"Get it off! Get if off!" Tanner yelled as he thrashed about in the van. He moved his hand to the lizard's throat and started to squeeze, slowly pulling it off his mangled, bloody hand.

The creature opened its jaws for a moment, then clamped them shut again, biting down harder on the raw wound. Tanner screamed, regained his grip, and pulled as hard as he could. It finally slipped off of his hand, removing a shredded strip of skin that now hung from the corner of its mouth. He tried to hold onto it, but it was so slick with blood that it easily slipped from his hands, dropping to the floor and scurrying toward the seats at the front of the van.

"Tanner!" Steve yelled. "What happened? Holy crap, you're bleeding all over the place!" He shot a look back at Ju. "What did you do to him?"

Ju held up her hands as a show of her complete innocence. Still, she couldn't hide her secret delight, and her smile grew larger as she watched the chaos unfold.

Tanner moaned, staring down at his shredded hand. He tried to cover it with his other hand to stop the blood, but it wouldn't stop. It hurt to touch it. He could see the bones of his hand through the cuts, felt his heartbeat in it as it pumped his life into and through the fresh wounds.

Tanner moaned again. "Ohhhh...." h said, closing his eyes. "I don't...I don't feel so good..."

"Don't worry," Ju said, leaning closer to him. "You won't feel much of anything in a few more minutes."

Tanner sighed, visibly exhausted. "Wh...why did you have a gecko in your backpack? That..." he paused, his breathing becoming more labored. "That...really hurt!" He closed his eyes, then shot open again as he fought for consciousness.

"Oh, that wasn't a gecko," Ju said with a smile. "That was Snapdragon. My pet Komodo."

"Komodo...?"

"As in komodo dragon?"

Tanner shook his head, not comprehending.

"You might have seen one at the zoo. Usually they're about five feet long, but Snapdragon's special. Grandma called him a 'dwarf komodo' or something. He won't get much bigger than my arm, she says."

"What's…what's happening to me?" he slurred, leaning back into his chair and resting his eyes. They were getting so heavy.

Ju beamed. "Oh, that? That's just his saliva coursing through your veins," she said, giggling. "Cool thing about Snapdragon? His spit's *super* poisonous. It's like, really, *really* bad."

Tanner wrinkled his brow, moaning loudly again as he shifted in his chair.

"In fact," Ju continued, "they say there's something like fifty different bacterial strains in their saliva. Seven of which are highly septic." She leaned in closer, her smile disappearing. "Four of which have no known antidotes."

Tanner's eyes rolled up into his head as he slumped forward and fell to the floor, sprawled out in a growing pool of his own blood. Ju moved her legs to the side so she wouldn't get splattered, then leaned forward again, studying his face.

"Good-bye, Tanner," she said coldly. "Never should've slapped me. Jerk." She extended her leg and kicked him in head, then sat back quickly when she saw Steve was pulling the van to the side of the highway.

"What…!" he exclaimed, looking at Tanner and the growing circle of blood underneath him. He shot a furious look at Ju. "No, no, no! This isn't happening. This is *not* happening!" he screamed, fumbling with the fanny pack at his waist. In a second he pulled out a small caliber pistol and aimed it at Ju.

"Start talking, you brat! What did you do to him?" he demanded, wagging the gun at her.

"I...I didn't do anything," Ju protested. "You saw me! I was back here, buckled in the whole time."

Steve looked at her, down at Tanner, and back to her. "No way. No freaking way." He pointed the gun at her head. "Start talking or I swear, I'm gonna—"

Before he could finish his sentence, a mouthful of razor sharp teeth sliced into the back of his calf from beneath his seat. Steve screamed and started to kick wildly behind him. As he reached down to grab his leg, he inadvertently squeezed the trigger on the pistol. There was a muted POP! and the windshield was suddenly sprayed with a fine mist of red as he shot a hole through the middle of his other hand. The driver's side window shattered, glass falling everywhere.

Steve dropped the gun and screamed louder. With his good hand he reached down and yanked hard on the green tail he could see, a bite-sized chunk of his calf coming with it. Even as he threw the demonic beast toward the back of the van, he caught a glimpse of it eagerly swallowing the bloody mouthful with an energetic gulp.

He fumbled with the door handle, kicked it open and jumped outside, screaming the entire time. Ju unbuckled herself and ran forward to lock the doors when she heard the sudden screeching of tires, followed by a THUMP! Through the bloody windshield she watched as Steve's lifeless body did an eerie, slow-motion cartwheel in the air, only to abruptly land on the pavement with a muffled thud.

The activity outside the van picked up with more screeching, a distant crash and a fresh collection of screaming. Ju stood up, walked over to her backpack and reached inside. She felt around until she found the concealed pocket on the side seam, retrieving her second cell phone. She turned it on, hit speed dial, and held it up to her ear.

It rang once and her mother answered. "Ju? Where are you? Are you okay?"

"Mom, I'm...okay." She touched her cheek again, determined to fight back the tears. Even then, her hand still shook with a mixture of outrage and terror.

"I was so worried! When you didn't come home I called Tim and Denny, but they didn't answer..."

"I know, Mom. But I'm fine. I'll be fine. I promise."

"Thank God," her mother gushed. "But where *are* you? Do you know where you are?"

"I'm...on the inner loop somewhere," Ju said, opening the side door. "Near the place Daddy plays golf? Desert Pines, I think? Hold on, I'll send you a pin on the map app. Just a sec..." She fiddled with the phone for a second, then brought the phone back to her ear. "There. You got it?"

A pause. "Okay...yes. We have it. We'll be there in a few minutes, hon. Don't go *anywhere*."

"Don't worry, Mom. I'll stay right here."

She stepped out of the van, lowered her hand to the floor and made a high-pitched clicking sound.

"Okay, baby. I love you."

"Yep. Love you too, Mom. Bye." She hung up and stuck the phone in her pocket. Lowering her head, she peered into the back of the van and clicked again.

"Hellooooo?" she sang. "It's okay. You can come out, now. They're dead."

A few seconds later, the reptile crawled out from the back of the van and cautiously placed one claw onto her palm. Ju beamed.

"That's a good boy! Now come here and give mommy a kiss!" she said excitedly. "Come on, now! Come on up!"

The dragon scampered up her arm to rest on her shoulder. Ju turned her head, closed her eyes and pursed her lips at him. He hesitated but a moment, then darted his head forward, giving her a quick, blood-stained kiss on the lips.

Ju giggled, placed a hand on his head and nuzzled him into her neck.

"I love you, Snapdragon," she whispered.

AUTHOR'S NOTE:

This is one of my all-time favorite stories, primarily because the way it came about was unlike any other story I've ever written. My wife and I serve as dorm parents at an international school, and one day one of our kids was making Snickerdoodle cookies. She commented how much she loved the word, and I shared that my favorite word was "Snapdragon," partially because of its sound but primarily because of the imagery it elicits when you say the word aloud.

Seriously. Say it for me. *Out loud.*

"Snapdragon."

Whether you scream it or whisper it, the word reverberates in your head. *Snapdragon.* I love it.

Anyhow, after I talked about it, I started thinking about how much fun it would be to write a short story with that title. So the next day I grabbed a drawing pad, some colored pencils, and within thirty minutes I had mapped out the setting, characters, scene order and some key dialogue. I wrote it in one sitting the very next day.

That act of raw, passionate creation was one of the most thrilling experiences of my life, and I have to say, I'm really happy with the way it turned out. What can I say? I love writing short stories!

END OF THE RAINBOW

The relentless Las Vegas wind bore against the army of consumers as they fought for the warm sanctuary of the mall. Once inside, the chaotic crowd darted aimlessly in frantic efforts to make their last-minute purchases for friends and loved ones. *Four days left.* There were a mere four days before the prices the stores blasphemously called "sales" would perish after Christmas Day. Until then, shoppers and vendors alike had to contend with the growing tidal wave of gift-giving procrastinators.

Stationed faithfully at every possible entrance was an ubiquitous Salvation Army Santa Claus, clanging his bell as loudly as possible in a fairly successful attempt at deafening those within earshot. Parents especially suffered at the Red Baron's torturous ringing, dragged closer by wide-eyed children eager to sit a spell on Santa's knee (only to find him again later inside the mall, where you had to pay to talk to him.) But most children, given their innate sense of deception, soon realized that the man at the door was simply one of Santa's "helpers." Someone who needed money to help feed the poor and wasn't really all that interested in what some little snot wanted for Christmas. Truth be told, the ringing Santas were probably too busy to even care if they were naughty or nice.

Both parents and children alike were shocked so

see a Santa casually walking among them in within the mall's halls. He was a tall, lanky Santa Claus, and much more disheveled than his jolly contemporaries. Although his suit consisted of the trademark electric red fluff, the white trim around it was horribly stained an off-putting, yellowish hue. His fake beard barely clung to his face, and the stocking cap/wig combination slumped lazily in front of his face rather than being posed gracefully to the side. Everyone around him quickly reached a common consensus; he was, without question, the most pathetic Santa Claus they had ever seen in their lives.

Swinging his Salvation Army bucket in one hand and closely clutching a wrapped present in the other, Santa walked between them with a half-hearted grin. Occasionally he would let out a boisterous "Ho, Ho, Ho!" as he passed terrified toddlers, squeezing their parents' hands tighter in his wake. Some would have mistakenly surmised he was drunk out of his mind, except for the sureness of his steps and direction.

As he neared the center courtyard of the mall, his pace slackened. He glanced down at his package, with its cherry red wrapping and taut, evergreen bow. It was admittedly a pathetic job of wrapping, but he reassured himself that it wasn't half bad for an old man. In the middle of the courtyard stood the gigantic Westdale Mall Christmas Tree, smothered in silver tinsel and lights and a variety of garish decor, somehow meant to arouse feelings of comfort and joy in the casual observer.

It made him want to throw up.

Nonetheless, the holiday had proved surprisingly useful to him, and he was happy to see how everything had worked itself out so smoothly this time. Just as he had planned it.

He casually pushed his way through the shifting wall of people to the base of the tree, smothered by a massive collection of presents in all shapes and sizes, each stacked neatly among the other in a large diameter. He grinned, estimating there were at least a hundred different presents before him.

He scanned the crowd for a moment, then stepped over the miniature, white picket fence that kept curious kids from trotting up and tearing into the empty boxes. His plan was perfect. Everyone this side of the North Pole knew that each and every elegantly-wrapped present stuck under this tree had exactly the same gift inside it. A great big box of *nothing*.

Every present, that was, except his.

He shuffled across the cotton-covered floor and gently lodged his present in with the others, nestling a few others on top of it to help it blend in. Carefully stepping back out of the collection, he complimented himself on his choice of location. He chuckled, his belly actually shaking for a few seconds. Granted, no one in their right mind was going to ask Santa Claus what he was doing staring at a bunch of presents in the middle of a mall, but he wasn't about to take chances. He'd made it this far, and he wasn't about to blow it now.

After straddling the fence he continued to walk aimlessly down the mall corridors, nodding jovially at his admirers as he secretly cursed them under his breath. Just a little farther and he was home free.

Across from him he saw the Shield Bank and

Trust lobby, surrounded by a growing fleet of police officers, guns drawn. He frowned, watching them scurry about like ants, confused and frightened shoppers running in his direction. Whatever was happening over there, he didn't want any part of it. He turned on his heels and fell into step with the flooding throng.

It was then that he noticed the two policemen ahead of him. His pace slowed as fear began to flooded his thought. Was it just his imagination, or were they making their way toward *him*? But why? Did they figure it out? How could they have possibly known He froze and slowly began to back away as they drew closer, never breaking eye contact.

He tried to make himself as small as possible, cursing at his failed attempt to blend into the crowd while wearing the most brightly colored, recognizable suit of the season. Then his worst fear came true.

"Hey!" one of them yelled. "Santa! Stop right there!"

The other policeman began to draw his weapon and started to sprint toward him.

Santa turned around and ran, violently shoving bumbling shoppers to the ground as he burst through them. Oversized black boots painfully weighted his every step as he tore through the crowd. "Move! Move it!" he yelled as he forced his way down the nearest escalator. A high school punk wearing a letter jacket tried to stop him at the bottom, only to find himself knocked flat on his back by Santa's holiday haymaker.

Just as he was nearing the exit he was tackled

from behind, his stocking cap flying off and landing gracefully on the floor a few feet ahead of him. "Get off me! Get off!" Santa screamed as he swung his empty change bucket over his head, hoping to connect with his assailant. His left arm was seized by the second policeman and wrenched painfully behind his back.

"Stop resisting!" the man yelled, struggling to clasp the handcuffs around his wrists. "Don't make us tase you!"

"Stop! I didn't do nothin' wrong!" Santa yelled back, free arm flailing in front of him. Horrified parents scooped up their children and fled out the exit, shielding their curious eyes from the scarring scene unfolding before them. There would be many creative, desperate explanations made about Santa Claus in Las Vegas that night.

Oblivious of his growing publicity, Santa thrashed fitfully on the mall floor as the two policemen wrestled with his other wrist.

"No! Let me go!" he yelled. "It's not fair! Let me go!"

"You have the right to remain silent!" the older officer shouted back, digging his knee between Santa's shoulder blades.

"Aaahhhh!"

"...anything you say can and will be used against you in—"

"Okay, okay! I'll talk! I'll tell ya everything you wanna know! OW! Cut it out!"

"Anything you say can and will be used against you..."

Santa started laughing, straining under the weight

of the other man as he slapped his wrist into the other handcuff, pinching off a piece of skin as he closed them.

"Aaaahhh! You pig! You did that on purpose! I'm gonna sue!"

Santa continued with his insane rants, kicking the air wildly as the two officers raised him to his feet and ushered him away. Nearby children continued to stare in fascination and fear as Santa Claus, the embodiment of all their holiday hopes and dreams, was carted away to spend the first night of his next ten years in jail.

○   ○   ○

George Dalton had worked as of the head janitor for the Westdale Mall for the past fourteen years, thoroughly enjoying the graveyard shift for the past five. It may be surprising, but most people simply aren't cut out for nighttime work. Either their bodies can never fully adjust to the time shift, or they have a spouse who absolutely refuses to sleep alone. George, on the other hand, had neither of these problems, which made the transition that much easier.

He especially enjoyed not having to ever hear that godforsaken, daily page, "Janitor to the food court!" which, loosely translated, meant "Hey, George! Some kid dropped their milkshake again!" It was only now, working at night, when the mall was dead and only a skeleton crew of janitorial zombies walked the floors that George was finally at peace.

He knew other people looked at it as a lowly position, but he didn't care. Frankly, he was darn good at keeping things clean; it was a skill he took pride in. Indeed, sometimes he felt it was an innate talent that he had actually been born with unlike most custodial workers who regarded their jobs as the final, depressing swirl in the toilet bowl of their lives. Those were the ones who had to be carefully trained to understand and appreciate the finer techniques of cleaning and disinfection. Whereas, George...well, George just *knew*.

He had just finished wiping down the display windows of The Gap when he saw Lester Dermont unlocking the front doors. He looked at his watch. Six forty-five already? A smile formed on his lips and he sighed. Time flies when you're having fun, I guess. He picked up the spray bottle and rags and made his way back to the stock room. He hoped the others were ready to wrap it up. That is, if they weren't screwing around again.

"Hey, George!"

The greeting startled him. He turned his head to see Mr. Dermont walking toward him briskly. Lester Dermont was the manager of the Westdale Mall, had been ever since his father, multimillionaire Lloyd Dermont, gave it to him as a belated birthday present a few years ago. Lloyd wanted to own every mall in the state of Nevada, with Westdale being the informal testing ground. It was a paltry, half-hearted gift in comparison to what he had given his other sons, but he figured it might help him prove to Lester once and for all that the kid just wasn't cut out for mall management.

Lester, on the other hand, was eagerly determined to prove his father wrong and went to great lengths keeping a tight rein on everyone who worked for him, exercising what little authority he had to a dictatorial degree.

George frowned. He never really liked the man and had no intention to start tonight. In his heart he quietly resented young punks who never learned the discipline of actually having to work for a living. Lester Dermont was the punk of the month.

"Good morning, Mr. Dermont," George replied, forcing a meager smile to his lips. Dermont ignored him.

"George, you heard about what happened today, right?"

"Yes, sir. Some kinda robbery gone wrong over at the bank?"

"Right. So you know it made quite a mess, do you?"

George nodded. "Yes, sir, and I assigned the job to Tyler first thing last night. Right when we first clocked in—"

"I need you to clean it again," Lester interrupted.

A worried expression fell across George's face. "What? I don't understand..."

"I need you to clean it again, George," Lester said, folding his arms cross his chest and leaning closer. He often did this an attempt to intimidate those he lectured at, but because he towered at a whopping 5'4", he typically failed.

George lowered his head a little and looked him in the eye. "I heard what you said, Mr. Dermont. I just don't understand why it needs to be done again.

Did he not clean it as I told him to?"

"No, he didn't."

George's face flushed.

"Well, he *did*," Lester corrected, "but it was a piss-poor job, so it needs to be done again before you go."

"Absolutely. I'll—"

"You tell Tyler that if he's ever that sloppy again? He's fired, you got that?" His cold stare bore into Dalton's forehead. "And another thing, George. If you can't keep your workers on task, I'm going to have to find someone who can. Understand me?"

George dug his hands deeper into his pockets to keep them from wrapping around Dermont's skinny, arrogant neck. "Yes, sir. I do. I understand perfectly."

"Good."

"Was there anything else, sir?" George asked.

Lester frowned at him as if had offered him a dead rat for a snack. "What? No. Just...go clean it up already!"

Satisfied with his short speech, Mr. Dermont turned and continued walking down the barren path of shops, his shoes slapping the tiles with annoying clarity.

George closed his eyes and sighed deeply. He had always liked his previous supervisors, but he didn't feel anything but contempt for Lester Dermont. He gathered his cart and slowly made his way to the bank lobby across the mall.

An hour and forty-five minutes later, George's

temper was slightly soothed by the frigid winter air as he walked out to the expansive parking lot which was slowly beginning to swell with the next desperate wave of customers. He rummaged around in his pocket for his keys as he approached his car, determined not to let his little run-in with Lester keep him from getting a solid day of rest. Just as he was about to open the door, he noticed a young man parked two cars down wrestling violently with the side door of his van. The youth let out a number of hushed expletives as he tugged vainly at the stuck door. In a sigh of disgust he struck the door and glanced over at George, as if suddenly realizing he was making a scene.

George turned away and was about to insert the key in his car's door when the young man called out to him.

"Hey! Hey, can you help me out here, mister?"

George looked over at him. His thick, black hair was slicked back and peppered with the light snow that had begun to fall. George glanced up at the sky. A white christmas in Vegas? The first one he'd seen in *his* lifetime.

Glancing back at the kid, it was clear his eyes communicated a hopeful plea. George shrugged. "What seems to be the problem?" he asked, walking over to him.

"The damn door froze on me again! I've been trying to open it for ten minutes now, and it won't budge. I thought maybe if we both tried it, it might give or something." He reached back and scratched the back of his head, forcing a meager smile.

"It's worth a try," George said, shrugging again.

"I'm afraid I'm not very strong, but I'll see what I can do." He gripped the frozen handle with both hands and began to tug backwards. The young man stood closely beside him and tried prying the door loose with his fingers.

"That's okay," he said, grinning. "To be honest, we don't really need you for your muscles."

"I'm sorry?" George asked, shooting him a quizzical look over his shoulder. The van door immediately swung open, and he was pulled inside and thrown to the back. He looked up in fear at the large, bearded man who had thrust him so effortlessly to the floor. The younger one jumped in quickly and shut the door behind him, breathing heavily.

"What? What is this? What's going on here?" George demanded as he rose to his feet.

"Sit down, old man!" the young one snapped, pushing him back down. His desperate features had now melted into a face hard-pressed for compassion, his eyes reflecting a cold, determined hatred. The larger one sat back in his chair and casually folded his arms across his massive chest, staring at him.

George looked at both of them and scooted back to the closest corner. He reached behind him and removed his wallet. "Here, just take it...I don't want any trouble." He slid it across the floor to them.

The large one picked it up and handed it over to the other, who now sat in a small chair beside him. "Thanks anyway, pops, but we're not here for money. Well...not *yours*, anyway."

"I...I don't understand."

"We need you to do us a favor."

"A what? A *favor*? I don't..."

The kid held his hands up to silence him. "It gets a little complicated so listen close, 'cause I ain't gonna repeat it, alright?"

George nodded quickly.

"So, yesterday was kind of a crazy day to be a Santa Claus at the mall, right?"

George nodded again. "Right. The bank robbery—"

"Exactly. But we didn't have anything to do with that crap. Thing is, as the cops were cleaning house grabbing every Santa they could see, they happened to nab a friend of ours." He paused to make sure George comprehended everything he had said.

"Anyhow," he continued, "Our little racket of impersonating the bell ringers was done with. We made pretty good money for a while there. Two, sometimes three thousand a day between the three of us. Problem was, most of it was in change, which makes it real hard to count at the end of the day, much less split." He sat back and sunk his hands into his baggy jeans, staring at the floor as he collected his thoughts. He nodded toward the larger man.

"Me 'n' Chuck here were never really good with numbers and all, so we told Mickey to roll the stuff up and exchange it for bills. Well, he weren't too happy about that at first, but he wasn't about to say no. I mean, let's face it. Not too many people say no to Chuck."

The large man continue to frown at George.

"Least, not more than once. Tends to make him kinda mad." He flashed a smirk toward Chuck. "So, Mickey was supposed to bring the money with him, and we'd split it when we got home. Thing is, he got busted before we could do that, which created a couple of problems for us. One, Chuck 'n' I didn't get our money, and two, Mickey decided to rat on us. The jerk told the cops it was all our idea; can you believe that?"

"But what does this have to do with me?" George blustered, "I don't—"

Chuck reached over and slapped him hard across the face. George let out a cry and backed into the corner.

"Yeeahh," the young one chuckled. "Chuck doesn't really like people interrupting me, either." He looked down at his shoes and smiled.

"Of course, we knew Mickey would squeal on us if he ever got the chance. He never was much of a team player, really. We figured the cops would be comin' by his apartment soon, so we decided we'd better beat them to it. When we got there his girlfriend was just headin' out the door, bags packed and everything. She wasn't expecting us; I could tell that when she saw us. She was like a deer in headlights or somethin'."

"When we asked where the money was, she tried acting dumb at first. Chuck changed her mind pretty quick, though, an' soon she told us how her an' Mickey were gonna start a new life together on the money we'd made. She swore she didn't know where Mickey had hid the money, but a few taps from Chuck's…ah…lie detector…made sure she was tellin' the truth. All she knew was he had left for the mall yesterday morning wearin' his Santa suit again and carryin' a present with him."

68

He stopped and sat up slowly, pulling two wrinkled scraps from his coat pocket. One was a glossy, red piece of paper while the other was a strip of dark, woodland green ribbon. He held them up for George to see.

"Found these in his trash can. Figure he probably knew Chuck 'n' I were gonna cut him out of his share, so he decided he'd keep the money with him, as insurance or something. Anyhow, all we know is he took the present inside with him but when they arrested him? He didn't have nothin'. Word is the only thing he was carryin' was his empty change bucket. Greedy punk was tryin' to score for one more day. Can you believe that?"

He handed the scraps over to George, who shied away for fear of getting hit again. After a moment the old man reached out a shaky hand and took them. He pretended to study them with intense interest.

"We're not exactly rocket scientists," the young man said. "But it don't take big brains to figure out where Mickey put the money, y'know? Probably sittin' under that stupid tree with every other freakin' present!" He snatched the scraps from George's trembling hands. "Pretty smart of him, really. Hidin' all that cash in the middle of a bunch of empty boxes. Who'd ever guess, y'know?"

George nodded. His butt felt cold, and his legs were starting to cramp up from sitting on the van's frigid floor.

"Anyhow," the youth said softly, "that's why we need you."

George glanced over at Chuck and swallowed slowly. He looked back at the young man, now raising his eyebrows in expectation.

"Yes?"

"I'm...sorry," George whispered. "I don't quite...understand."

"It's like this. We can't go in there 'cause, for all we know, our mugs are famous now. But we've been watching you for a few days now, right? An' you seem to be a regular customer 'round here. What are you anyways, a security guard?"

"I'm...the head custodian."

"Whatever. It's simple, right? We need you to go back in there an' bring out the box of bucks. Understand?"

George stared at him in disbelief. He wrung his hands together and closed his eyes slowly, turning his head to the right. "You...you want me to get the present for you, is that it?" he said, his voice quivering and faint.

The kid tapped Chuck with the back of his hand. "Hey, is this guy a genius or what?" Chuck ignored him.

George Dalton started to cry. It wasn't a loud, sobbing cry, but a quiet murmur, culminating with tears that slowly spilled from his eyes. He shook his head in denial. "I can't," he whispered quietly.

The young man's mouth opened slightly. "Whoa...hold on...*what* did you just say?"

George glanced over at Chuck and began to shake as if he were a child about to get a scolding for wetting the bed. "I...I can't do it," he wailed louder. He closed his eyes and braced himself for what he knew would follow.

The blow came from the left this time. When

George's head bounced off the van wall he could already taste the blood beginning to fill his mouth. He continued to sob as the two men stared at him from their chairs, unmoved. The young one sighed and looked down at George's wallet.

"So...George. Looks like you live over on Fennel Avenue, huh? Nice area of town." He look up at George and frowned. "Chuck 'n' I are gonna grab some breakfast and then I'm gonna meet you back here in an hour. If you're not there with the goods, or try anything funny like talking to the police?" He shook his head sadly. "Well, Chuck here will make sure you never talk to anyone again."

His body overcome with pain, George slowly pushed himself up to a sitting position, wiping his bloody mouth on the sleeve of his jacket. He raised his hands up in front of him in surrender. "Please, you don't understand, I'm..." Chuck's leg shot out and kicked him in the stomach. George curled up in a tight ball and cradled his abdomen, moaning in agony over his newfound pain.

"Nah, I think *you're* the one who don't understand, pops. If you don't get our money back? You're a *dead* man." He flipped open the wallet and took out some of the pictures, holding one up for George to see. "An' you won't be the only one."

"Please," he wheezed. "Don't hurt Anna. She's my only daughter, she's so precious..."

"Oh, yeah? Anna, huh?" His eyes lingered on the photo and he smiled. "Hm. Good-lookin' kid."

"Please..."

"Look, gramps. To be honest? We don't wanna hurt anyone. We don't. But we *do* want our money.

71

An' if we gotta kill a few people to get it? Well..." He shrugged innocently.

George nodded his head, moaning softly as he cradled his stomach.

The kid put the pictures back inside the wallet and slipped it into his coat pocket along with the scraps of paper. "So. We have ourselves a deal or what?"

George looked down at the dirty van floor. His shoulders shook uncontrollably as he silently broke down in front of them, the tears streaming down his wrinkled face, stinging his split lip.

"Yes. I'll do it," he finally whispered. "I'll do it."

The side door of the van thrust open, and he was shoved out onto the parking lot, now covered with a thin layer of snow. He crawled over to his car, feeling a small sense of relief as he heard the van driving away. A mixture of tears and blood began to crystallize over his swollen, anguished face.

His hands shook so violently that it still took him another two minutes before he could successfully open his car door, despite the fact that it was already unlocked. Exhausted, George fell into the seat and started the engine. As the heater fluttered to life and the air slowly began to grow warmer, he leaned his head back on the headrest and started to cry once more.

"You...you don't understand," he whispered between fervent gasps for breath. "I just can't do it. I'm...I'm colorblind."

As the soft falling snow continued to color the world a brilliant shade of white, George Dalton leaned his forehead onto the frigid steering wheel

and spent the next twenty minutes of his life crying
in his car.

KICKING AROUND

Click-click.

Scott lowered the camera and frowned.

"How do you think it got up there?" he asked.

"Haven't a clue," Dan grunted. They'd been stopped on the trail for a good five minutes, but he still couldn't look away from the tree. "I'd imagine it was probably dead well before it got stuck."

Scott scowled at him. "What makes you say that?" He pulled a thermos out of his backpack and took a swig. The early morning climb had been his idea to begin with, but he still found himself somewhat winded as they walked the trail.

Dan jutted his chin toward the deer. "Check out the neck," he said.

"Yeah?"

"See how it's all dangly and lopsided?"

"Sure."

"I believe it broke its neck somehow," Dan said with a smug smile.

Scott looked at Dan, back at the deer, and back to Dan again. "And I think you're an idiot," he said.

"What? Why?"

"Because," Scott said slowly, "if a deer goes off and breaks its neck, it ain't gonna go climbin' up fifteen feet to die in a tree." He raised his camera and took three more shots. *Click-click-click.*

"Well, of course not," Dan protested. "But maybe

a bobcat or mountain lion caught it, broke its neck in the process and stashed it up there. You know, for a midnight snack or something."

"Are you serious?"

Dan grinned. "What? They do stuff like that. I think I saw it on *Animal Planet* or something."

"Uh-huh."

"Dude. It so could've happened that way."

Scott took another drink, swished the water around in his mouth and spat it out on the trail. "No, dorkus," he said, shaking his head. "It couldn't have. Especially not like that."

"What? Why the heck not?" Dan was losing his patience. They'd been close friends for two years and college roommates for one, but today Scott was seriously beginning to get on his nerves. It was the name-calling. It was immature and annoying, and he was starting to get angry.

"Because," Scott jeered.

"Because *why?*"

"Becaauuse…" Scott intoned, pointing to the deer, "of the way that one branch is stickin' out of the middle of its gut." He held up the camera and zoomed in closer, capturing the exquisite details of the blood-crusted puncture wound. *Click-click.*

Dan moved up the trail to get a better look. Scott was right. A bloody, 3-foot branch was jutting directly out of the animal's rib cage, pointing upward at an awkward angle. "So…?"

"So, you think a mountain cat's somehow able to grab the thing by the neck, haul it up the tree, and drop it with enough force to impale it on that thing? And at that angle?"

Dan studied the tree, doing the calculations in his mind. He slowly shook his head. "Nope," he finally exclaimed, "You're right. There's no way a cat could've done that." He looked up the trail, studying the ground. "Maybe a bear?" he shrugged. "You know, they're a lot stronger than they look. Smarter, too."

"As opposed to you? The 'bear with very little brain?'" Scott said, sneering at him. "Nah, it wasn't a bear..."

"Well, what was it then, hotshot? You're the outdoorsman. What's *your* theory? One of Santa's frequent fliers? Did he lose his happy thoughts up in the sky? Fall down go boom?"

Scott laughed. "Ah, I don't know. I just think it's cool." He looked up through his camera again. *Click-click.* "Kinda creepy, all crushed and shish-ka-bob'd, but still pretty cool."

Dan shook his head. "Well, creepy's a good word for it." He reached behind his back and patted one of the pockets on his backpack. "Still, I'm glad I brought along the bear repellent."

Scott lowered the camera and stared at him blankly.

"You know...just in case?" Dan said.

Scott hung his head and shook it slowly. "Dan...dude...you really are kind of hopeless out here, you know that?"

Dan bristled. "And why's that?"

"'Cause I've been hiking and climbing out here for the past three months, and aside from a few rabbits and Blitzen here," he jerked a thumb at the deer above them. "I ain't seen *jack*. Much less a big bad bear."

"Still," Dan sniffed in defiance, "you realize that this place has the fifth largest grizzly population in North America…"

"Oh, here we go…" Scott murmured, placing his camera's lens cap on and stuffing it back into his backpack.

"…so the chances of a bear attack are higher here than anywhere else because…"

"Wait. *Fifth largest?* Are you being serious, now?"

"It's true."

Scott raised his hands in mock surrender. "Fine…. You win, Encyclopedia Brown. Man, you can be such a downer sometimes…" Slinging his backpack back over his shoulders, he started back up the trail. "Let's go already," he called behind him. "We're burning up daylight, and it's only gonna get hotter."

Dan took one last look at the deer, shook his head, and fell in step behind him. Despite the distraction, he couldn't shake the feeling that this day was only going to continue its slow and steady descent into sucking.

A half hour later they were scaling the cliff face, slowly making their way to the top. Dan had to hand it to him; Scott really was an expert climber, and he had secured the gear in such a way that even a novice like himself could make the climb without feeling like he was going to slip and splatter on the ground twenty feet below.

Dan looked up just as Scott disappeared over the ridge, carelessly kicking dust and rubble down on him.

"Hey! Watch it!" he yelled, ducking to avoid getting it in his eyes or mouth.

"Hey. Sorry about that, man!" Scott's head appeared above him. "I guess I got pretty excited, once I reached the top."

Dan sighed. "Just…please watch where you're—"

"Awesome!" Scott interrupted, staring out at the forest. "You should check out this view! Just unreal!"

"Wait. Haven't you seen it before?"

"Not from this one. This is my first time up this side of the rock. I usually tackle the east side instead. Thought I'd go easy on you. You know, being your first time and all."

"Um…thank you?"

"You bet, buddy," he said, disappearing once again.

Great, Dan thought. *I'm stuck on the side of a mountain I've never been on, and my "guide" hasn't even been here before to scope it out.* He shook his head. First the deer, and now this? *If this is how the day's going so far,* he thought, *this isn't going to end well.*

He clung to the ropes a little bit tighter, even though he knew they were secure enough that even if he dropped, he probably wouldn't fall more than a few feet. Or so he hoped. He studied the wall above him, trying to determine the path Scott had taken. From his viewpoint, he couldn't see a decent handhold whatsoever.

"Hey!" he yelled, "Wanna give me a hand down here?"

"Just a second…" Scott yelled from the distance.

"Just a…!" Dan fought back the urge to scream.

"I'm kind of stuck, here! Could use a little help? Hello?"

"Hold onto your panties! I'm setting up the camera…"

Dan frowned. "Wait. Hold on. You're doing what, now?"

"The camera? Hello? I'm setting it on my tripod, so I can catch this awesome view. Gonna put it on panorama mode, let it microburst every ten seconds to get this awesome sunrise."

Dan closed his eyes in frustration. Ever since Scott received the new camera for his birthday last month, he'd been obsessed with it, taking photos of everything and everyone he could, everywhere he went. He was constantly exploring the numerous features and settings on it. The guy would spend hours just reading through the manual. Typically out loud, much to Dan's dismay.

He swore. Dan *knew* he never should have agreed to come out here. He wasn't an outdoor guy. *At all.* One hellish week of camping with his family back in high school was enough confirm of this. Sure, he liked the *idea* of s'mores, socializing by the fire, roasting hot dogs and the like. But the reality was he'd rather spend that time reading a good novel squirreled away in an isolated corner of the RV.

More rustling up above, and he looked up just in time to get another face full of dirt.

"Hey! STOP IT!"

Scott's face popped over the edge again. "Sorry, I'm sorry…I just wanted to let you know the camera's all set."

"That's great. Now would you please…"

"Be right back. I gotta go take a dump."

"What? No! No, Scott!" Dan yelled. "Take your dump later! I've been hanging here for over ten minutes! TEN MINUTES!"

"Dude, I'll just be three minutes, tops…" and he disappeared again. "I'm gophering, man! Have some pity!" he yelled as he dropped out of sight.

"HEY!" Dan yelled again, his voice strained with exasperation. He looked out over the forest canopy and glared at the scenic sunrise.

Three minutes passed. Then another three. After eight minutes Dan decided he wasn't going to wait around for Scott's help anymore. He didn't want it. The jerk wasn't going to get the satisfaction of helping him "conquer the great outdoors" for another minute. In fact, not only was he planning to finish the rest of climb on his own, but once he got topside? He was going to throw down his backpack and beat the living snot out of the guy. Frankly, he didn't care if their friendship survived after that. This was it. He'd had enough.

After a series of grunts, serious straining, and two failed attempts, Dan finally found a viable purchase point for his hand and pulled himself close enough to the edge to prop a foot over it. Flexing every muscle he had, he pulled himself up to the plateau, rolling to his side in the dirt. Out of breath, his chest heaving in and out as he struggled for oxygen, he stared up through the trees at the pastel sky.

Dan was furious.

But he did have to admit that the view over the forest floor *was* pretty impressive, even for a non-nature lover like himself.

Two minutes passed, and Dan finally stood up, squirming out of his backpack and tossing it angrily to the ground. He unhooked the rope from his harness and dropped it to the ground where it bounced and promptly disappeared over the edge.

Dan scrambled to grab it, but stopped himself just before he plunged over the edge. He lay on the ground, staring at the rope as it swung from the nearest hook, three feet away. Well out of arm's reach. *That's great,* he thought, pushing himself to his feet. *Freaking fan-TAS-tic.*

"Hey!" he yelled. "What's the matter with you? You left me hanging on a cliff, you know!"

He scanned the area, but all he saw was dense forest to his right, a collection of large boulders to the left and Scott's gear in a heap a few feet away. Beside it, the camera was fixed atop a thin tripod, a faint *CLICK* emitting from it every few seconds. Dan's first instinct was to drop his pants and moon it, but then he calculated the power of the Internet combined with an eternal, digital image, and decided against it. His computing professor's wise words echoed in the back of his mind. *Once it's online, it's out there forever.*

Instead he glared at it, sticking out his tongue. *Dumb camera,* he thought, looking around again. He picked up a rock and chucked it at it, missing by at least three feet. *Whatever.*

"Scott!" he yelled, walking toward the forest. "I swear, if this is some kind of a joke just to scare me on camera, you're gonna…"

Snap.

Dan stopped moving, turning his head toward the

sound, straining to listen. He could have sworn he heard something, but now there was nothing but silence. He was about to take a step when he heard a muffled rustling over to his left, just behind the boulders. He slowly stepped toward it, ear cocked to hear better.

More rustling, followed by a grunt. Dan smiled. *Found you, dork.*

"Let me just say, you had better be making a colossal poop, buddy," Dan said as he strolled around the corner. "Because that is the *only* reason I'm not going to…"

Dan froze.

He stared down at the ground where Scott lay, staring up at him, unmoving. His eyes were wide open, his face frozen in a look of unmistakable terror. His head jerked to the side an inch, and Dan's eyes slowly moved down Scott's corpse, coming to rest at the black creature still hunched over him.

It's back to him, Dan watched as the blood-soaked bear tore violently into Scott's torso, burying its muzzle deeper into the open ribcage. Dan stood paralyzed, his body refusing to move even as his mind recoiled in horror. *Snap!* The familiar sound split the air as the bear bit into another one of Scott's ribs, snapping it off effortlessly.

Unfortunately, that was the moment Dan's body finally caught up with his mind, but instead of running away he found himself doubled over, violently vomiting his morning's protein-rich breakfast bar onto the ground directly in front of him. He tried to cover his mouth to prevent it from coming out, but he couldn't stop himself. It flooded through his fingers, the chunk-filled, burning bile splattering everywhere.

As the last few globs fell from the corner of his mouth, he looked up slowly. The bear had now turned around and its eyes locked on his, a bloody rib extending awkwardly from the corner of its mouth. It bit down on it with a loud *crunch*, stopped chewing, and let out a low, guttural growl.

Dan slowly stepped backwards, hands raised, palms outward, in what he had read would be a universal attempt to avoid provoking wild animals. As soon as he was out of a direct line of sight, he turned and sprinted toward the cliff.

OhGodImDeadOhGodImDeadOhGodImSoDead...

For a second he considered jumping off the edge of the cliff. A quick, plummeting death would be far more preferable to facing off with a bear or having his ribs ripped from his chest, one by one. Then he remembered the bear spray he had bragged about earlier.

Falling to his knees, he had just begun to unzip the pocket when he saw the bear amble around the corner of the rock, fifty feet away.

Dan froze. *Maybe he won't see me. Maybe he has really bad eyesight. Maybe he'll...*

The bear turned and stared directly at him.

Crap.

The bear roared loudly, but didn't move, staring at him from the edge of the forest. Dan stared back, slowly reaching down and removing the noisy plastic wrap from the can. He kept his head straight, unmoving, stealing glances downward as he attempted to read the directions. Was he supposed to shake the dang thing before using it? Or was it good to go?

He looked up again just as the bear took a step forward, preparing to charge. Dan stood, extended his arm out in front and pressed down hard on the nozzle head.

Nothing happened.

He pressed it harder. There was a pathetic fizzle as the can's spout sputtered a yellowish solution onto his fingers and stopped. He shook the can furiously and tried again. Nothing happened.

Crap.

He threw the can at the approaching bear and was about to turn toward the cliff, mentally preparing to jump and try to grab the climbing rope when he suddenly stopped. Behind the bear, something had moved in the forest. Something...huge.

Dan stood still, frozen in fear.

Did that tree just move?

As the charging bear closed the gap between them, Dan watched in a mixture of horror and amazement as a gigantic creature emerged from the forest trees. As it moved, it suddenly let out a savage scream.

The bear stopped its forward attack and turned to face the new threat. Dan tried to understand what he was seeing. The creature was almost twenty feet tall, shockingly thin and covered with faded, greyish fur and what looked like pieces of bark.

What is *that thing?* Dan thought, staring into the forest. *It's huge! The thing's like a walking tree! With arms!*

As the creature approached them, Dan noticed

Scott's backpack to the right. He stared from the forest back to the bear and carefully started to move closer to it. Maybe...just maybe...there was something in it he could use to defend himself.

The bear let out a low growl as the creature drew nearer, then lowered its head and started to back up. It turned its head toward Dan, and they made eye contact. It was clearly terrified. As it took a few more cautious steps backwards, Dan watched it empty itself with each step, large clumps of poop strung across the ground around it. Whether it was a survival instinct or out of sheer fear, he didn't know.

The bear turned and darted toward the cliff just as the monstrous creature sprinted after it, moving faster than Dan thought could be possible for something so massive. Just as the bear leapt off reached the edge of the cliff and launched itself into the air, the monster's giant hand clamped around its neck and plucked it from the air, yanking it backwards and violently slamming it to the ground.

The bear yelped and tried to squirm out of his grip, but the creature punched it in the chest twice, breaking a number of its ribs and effectively taking the fight out of it.

The monster lifted the bear up by its neck until it hung limply in its hand, suspended ten feet in the air. Dan blinked, his mind rejecting what he was seeing. How was it even possible that something so tall and lanky was strong enough to pick up a bear one-handed? This was insane!

From off to the side, Dan watched as the two creatures stared into each other's eyes, the smaller one emptying its bladder as it hung helpless in the air. A second later the creature clamped his other giant hand over the bear's head and swiftly wrenched it to the side. Dan heard the distinct, sharp snap of bones and saw the bear's body become limp.

Using both hands, the monster pulled the dead bear up to its chest and squeezed, compressing the smaller creature repeatedly, turning it over and over in the process of making it symmetrically spherical. *He's making it into a ball*, Dan thought, wincing at the sound of multiple bones breaking. A dark stream of blood ran down the creature's arms, forming a misshapen puddle at its feet. An eyeball popped from one of the sockets and rolled across the ground, resting near Dan's feet.

What...is happening...?

Dan's head started spinning. He sank to his knees as he fought to retain consciousness. *This is impossible...this is a dream...I'm dreaming...I've gotta be dreaming...this can't be happening...*

A loud pop from another breaking bone snapped him from his stupor, and he watched the creature slowly stoop down near the edge of the cliff, carefully placing the compacted remains of the bear. In Dan's mind it looked somewhat like an oversized ball, albeit one composed entirely of fur, bones, and blood.

Dan froze as the creature rose to its full height, turned and walked past him back toward the forest. It ignored him completely, stopping only momentarily to scoop up some of the bear's feces along the way, popping the soft lumps into its mouth like they were candy. Dan's mind continued to implode on itself under the sheer weight of the morning's unrelenting horrors. The monster walked into the trees and disappeared from view, blending seamlessly into the trees with uncanny camouflage. Just before it vanished entirely, however, Dan saw it turn around. It stood there, motionless, staring back at the cliff.

Seconds later it made an odd panting sound, followed by a low, guttural growl. It took off running through the forest toward the cliff, a slender horror moving impossibly fast. Moments before it reached the edge, it slowed down, banked to the left and kicked the fur ball squarely in its center.

There was a sick, wet sound as the giant foot connected, and in the next instant the bear ball was launched over the forest canopy below, unraveling grotesquely as it sailed out of sight. The creature bellowed joyfully, turning to face Dan with a large grin spread across his face.

Dan sat frozen, petrified to move. He wished he were invisible, but the monster was clearly making some kind of an attempt to communicate with him. He slowly raised his hand and raised a thumb high.

"Uh..." he began shakily. "Good kick?"

The creature's grin vanished. It stomped over to where he cowered, crouching low and lowering its head even more until it was eye level. Dan didn't move. He simply stared back and started to cry. The creature's head was easily ten times the size of a human's. Softball-sized, black eyes bore into him, unblinking.

"And..." Dan stammered through his tears. "Th...thanks...for...uh...saving me?"

The creature said nothing.

Dan slowly stood up and waved a hand timidly. "I mean it. I...uh...really appreciate it." He nodded his head, afraid to say anything more.

The creature's head started to bob in tandem with his. A second later it chuffed at him, possibly in an attempt to laugh. Then it smiled. Dan's heart lurched inside him and he smiled back, trying to remember if he'd ever heard of any savage sightings mentioning a creature capable of smiling.

Dan laughed, nodding his head even more. He was wrong. This day didn't suck after all. In fact, he could easily envision a future where sucky days no longer existed for him. Ever.

The creature continued to grin at him as it casually reached over, wrapped a massive hand around him and lifted him off the ground.

Oh, crap.

Dan's arms were now pinned tightly against his body, and as the creature walked toward the cliff, swinging him beside itself, he felt one of his ribs snap from the pressure. He screamed in agony, his eyes wide at the terror of what was happening. At what he knew was *about* to happen.

The creature lifted him up toward his face, still grinning. Through his pain Dan was overwhelmed with the putrid breath washing over him, black bits of bear dung still stuck between a pair of yellowing fangs.

A hand suddenly reached over, came to rest on his head, and stopped.

"Please..." Dan begged. "Please, don't...I don't want to die...I just—"

There was a loud pop, and suddenly all of Dan's

pain vanished instantly. His head flopped limply to his shoulder, and he watched helplessly as the creature closed its hands over his body and started to crush it, rolling him over in its hands just as it had crumpled the bear not two minutes earlier.

An immense headache started to flood through Dan's temple as he was gingerly placed on the edge of the cliff, facing the forest. Through his one functional eye and his lopsided, pounding head, he watched as the creature strode away back into the forest once more.

Just as he felt himself fading, about to lose all consciousness, Dan heard a deafening roar and the ground beneath him started to shake. He could only stare straight ahead with his one good eye as the monster ran toward him with shocking speed, the weathered foot connecting with his broken body at the last possible second.

Dan died long before he hit the ground.

o   o   o

Thirty-six hours later...

"See, babe? I told you that you'd love it up here," Mark said, helping Stacy up and over the edge of the cliff. He stood back and looked out over the forest, appreciating the scenery as the sun began to set in the west. Mark smiled as he gestured over the cliff. "So, what do you think? Is this beautiful, or what?"

Stacy held his hand close and leaned her head on his shoulder. "It is," she whispered. "Thank you for bringing me here. I love it."

"I knew you would."

"And you were right."

They kissed and continued to admire the view for another few minutes, watching as the sky's glow slowly changed from faded blue to a spectacular pink and crimson combination.

Stacy shivered. "I'm getting cold. Can we please start setting up camp?"

"What? Oh, yeah. Sure thing." Mark started to take his backpack off. "We just need to find a good spot. Preferably one with a view, you know?"

"If you say so, *babe*," Stacy cooed. She pecked him on the lips again before she stepped back, looking at the spacious plateau behind them. The ground was soft with a fresh collection of pine needles, so finding a good place to erect a tent hopefully wouldn't be as difficult as she'd imagined.

As Mark was unpacking the tent, Stacy stopped walking and stared at the ground a few feet ahead, a look of confusion crossing her face.

"Honey?" she asked.

"Yep?"

"What is that?"

Mark stood up and looked at her. "What is what?"

She pointed. "There. On the ground."

He walked over and looked down at the ground, lightly kicking something with his shoe. A moment later he knelt down and picked the object up.

"Well, well," he exclaimed. "Looks like someone left a camera behind." He turned it over in his hands, wiping away the dirt and debris as he opened the tripod and stood it back up. "Darn shame, too.

'Cause this looks like a seriously expensive camera."

Stacy walked over to him and looked closer. "Maybe we can find who it belongs to? Do you see a name or anything on it?"

Mark shook his head. "No...but..." he reached over and pushed a button. There was a quiet beep, followed by a quiet whir as the lens opened. "...maybe we can find out who it belongs to by browsing their photos."

"Mark..."

"What?"

"Don't. It's invading their privacy."

"Stacy. Come on. I'm only trying to find whose it is, is all." He navigated to the photos and started browsing through them.

Stacy sighed and shook her head in disapproval. She thought about how much she would hate it if someone looked through her private photos, snapshots of her precious memories. She walked away and looked around the forest behind them. Just like the view behind her, she had to admit that the endless canopy of trees really was breathtaking. That was when she noticed the white golf ball on the ground a few feet away. She walked over toward it, annoyed that someone would ruin a perfectly secluded nature escape by bringing along their stupid sports equipment.

"Holy crap," Mark suddenly exclaimed.

She looked over her shoulder. "What?"

Mark stared at the camera, eyes wide. "Ho. Lee. *Crap.*"

"What? What is it?"

Mark looked up at her, his face changing from

one of shock to euphoria. "Baby, can you say 'Bigfoot?'" he said with a grin. "We are gonna be rich. Filthy, stinking *RICH*!"

Stacy frowned. She loved him, but sometimes his practical jokes got out of hand. Especially when they were at her expense. "Whatever..." she whispered. She turned around and reached for the ball, but stopped just short of touching it. She stooped down to get a closer look. She wasn't sure what, but there was something about it that wasn't... right.

"I'm serious!" Mark insisted, walking over to where she stood. "I'm telling you, the photos on this camera are worth a *fortune*!"

Stacy ignored him, using a nearby stick to brush aside the pine needles from the ball. A second later she froze, dropping it to the ground as an icy chill flooded into her veins, the blood draining from her face. She looked in terror at the lone eyeball staring back up at her from where it lay on the ground.

Without saying a word, she stood up, staring out at the forest once more. "Mark..." she whispered.

"*The National Enquirer. Time* magazine. Heck, maybe we'll even get invited on *The Daily Show*!" Mark gushed excitedly.

"Mark..." Stacy said quietly, eyes straining to understand what she was looking at, what was happening deep in the woods ahead of her.

"We can buy you a new car so you won't have to drive that crappy Toyota anymore...and..."

"*Mark*!" she hissed.

He stopped talking, finally looking up from the camera at her. He followed her gaze into the woods.

"What? What is it?"

He squinted, straining to see what she could possibly be gaping at.

A tear ran down her cheek as she stared straight ahead, transfixed. Slowly she raised her hand and pointed toward the forest.

"Did..." she whispered, "Did that tree just move?"

Author's Note

I chose to call this story "Kicking Around" only because it's got the double-meaning thing going on, with the laid-back hiking/climbing motif, and the fact that Bigfoot crushes his victims into a ball before he kicks 'em into oblivion. Get it? Kicking A Round? (Another suggested title was "Meatballs," which I also think would've worked.)

What can I say? I like to reward readers who pay attention to the small stuff.

Some of my beta readers commented on how gruesome it was, saying the story stuck with them long after they read it. I have to admit, this was never my intention. I've always wanted to write a Bigfoot story, and as I was writing it I kept asking myself "What would make this stand out from every other Bigfoot story that's been written? Maybe I should make him act like a savior? And face down a bear? Oh yeah, that'd be cool!"

PREDATORS

Prologues & Epilogues

The creature didn't stand a chance.

It was certainly fast. Scrambling over the stony ground, it had the muscular build of an animal that was well-accustomed to the rigors of everyday survival. Yet even as it pursued the smaller dinosaur just out of reach of its claws, it was clearly oblivious that it, too, was being hunted by a third, larger reptile close behind it.

If it was aware of the danger, the beast didn't show it. Tiny arms outstretched in a futile attempt to snatch its prey, solely focused on the succulent prize darting ahead of it. Perhaps it overestimated its ability to escape the final threat in time to enjoy its own conquest. Perhaps it just couldn't conceive of defeat, either of its own success or its personal safety. Regardless, the finality of the situation was clear to any casual observer.

The predator had become the prey.

The little girl reached out and placed a delicate hand on the center dinosaur's back, gently stroking its head, then tracing the multiple bumps down its slender spine until she reached the tip of the tail. She caressed it, rubbing the nub until it grew warm between her fingers. The bronze overlay was cold to her touch, but it accurately captured the three creatures in exquisite detail, and she relished the texture of the rough, reptilian skin as it brushed against the softness of her own.

Ju glanced back at her father, seated behind his desk in the center of the enormous office. He was busy shuffling a stack of papers, pausing only when he sensed her staring at him.

"Yes?" he mused, not looking up. "You have a question?"Ju beamed at him.

Joseph put his papers down and gave her his full attention. He could always sense when someone was looking at him, a gift that proved to be even more sensitive when it came to his daughter. "And?" he asked. "What is it, princess?"

"What does it mean?"

He frowned. "What does what mean?"

"This," she said, pointing to the sculpture. "The dinosaurs chasing each other."

Joseph smiled at her. "And what, may I ask, makes you think it has a deeper meaning?"

She turned around and started to stroke the head of the largest one, the Tyrannosaurus rex. Her eyebrows wrinkled across her forehead. "I don't know," she said, "I just…think it does."

Her father placed the papers down on his enormous desk, rose from his chair, and walked toward her. He stood beside her, staring at the sculpture in silence for a few seconds. "Tell me this, Ju. What do *you* think is happening here?"

"Well," she began, "The baby dinosaur is going out for a jog, and then the big brother is chasing it. And then it's being chased by an even *bigger* dinosaur." She glanced up at him. "A T. rex. Right?"

"That's correct," her father nodded. "But I don't believe they're brothers."

"No?"

He shook his head. "I'm afraid not. Plus, I think you missed something else."

"I did?"

He nodded. "Look closer at the smallest one. You might be surprised to see that he's not just jogging..."

She looked up at her father, then back to the sculpture. She bent down to study it closer, squinting to focus better. The baby reptile was clearly in motion, the legs beautifully shaped to show their strain as it lunged ahead of the other two. She looked back at her father and frowned.

"Look over here," Joseph said, pointing to a small patch of overgrowth in front of it. "You'll see it."

Ju inched closer and squinted even harder to see what he was pointing at. She was surprised and delighted when she saw that what she had originally thought to be a simple clump of grass now hid a fourth, even smaller creature on the run.

"A *baby* baby!" she squealed with delight.

Joseph laughed. "That's right. So, perhaps the baby behind it isn't as innocent as you thought it was, yes?"

"Okay. But what does it *mean*?"

He sighed. "Again with the meaning of things..."

"Well, you bought it for a reason, didn't you?" she asked, crossing her arms. Her smile had faded, replaced by a look of simmering annoyance.

"I did," he said, nodding. He reached out and placed his hand on the back of the T. rex, smiling. "When I saw this last year in Malaysia, it resonated with me. I instantly recognized that it was more than a simple sculpture. These creatures represent many aspects of life." Joseph frowned. "And death," he added. A sad look crossed his face and he slowly removed his hand.

"When I look at this," he continued, "I'm reminded that life is full of many different kinds of people. Some serve as little more than prey." He gestured to the smallest creature. "They're the smallest in the food chain, and they have to constantly move about from place to place just to survive. Yet even when you're the hunter, focused and intent on what's directly in front of you," he moved his hand to the center dinosaur, "you can't become too comfortable, because there's always someone bigger than you. A predator can easily become the prey if he's not protected from the world around him."

Ju stared at the sculpture without saying a word, eyes slowly moving from one creature to the other. After a few seconds she cocked her head to the side and looked back to her father. "Which one are you?" she asked.

He stared at the sculpture, taking a deep breath. "Well," he said, clearing his throat, "I suppose you could say I'm all three." He pointed to the smallest. "I started out as the little guy, with absolutely nothing. Then I worked for many, many years, expanding the business and actually making a profit." He gestured to the middle dinosaur. "Unfortunately, sometimes I have to do things in business that other people don't like. So there are always going to be those who see me as nothing more than a predator." He nodded to the T. rex. "The bad guy."

"But you're not, are you?"

"Not what? A bad guy?"

She nodded.

"No, honey. I'm not a bad guy. They just *think* I am."

Ju reached over and took his hand. "Well, you're good enough for me, so I think I'm gonna keep you."

"Why, thank you…I think…"

A faint chime sounded from behind them at his desk. "Mr. Cho?" a pleasant voice said over the intercom.

"Yes, Alice?" Joseph called, walking back toward his desk.

"Do you have a moment, sir? I just needed to review some things with you before you leave."

"Absolutely," Joseph said, sitting down. "Please come in."

A few seconds later the office door opened, and a short, middle-aged woman slipped into the room, smiling. "I do apologize for the intrusion, Mr. Cho…"

He waved a hand to the side. "Not a problem, Alice. How can I help you?"

"Well, sir, first I wanted to remind you that your lunch reservation at the Lucky Dragon is at one o'clock."

"The Lucky Dragon!" Ju said, jumping excitedly. "I love that place!"

"You do?" Alice said, smiling at her. "And what do you—"

"Tomorrow's my birthday!" Ju interrupted, beaming.

"Is it really?" Alice said, feigning ignorance. "Why, that's just fantastic! How old will you be?" she asked, winking at Joseph.

"Eight. And I'm getting a pony, aren't I, Daddy?"

"We'll talk about it later, dear," Joseph said, forcing a smile.

"I'd better get a pony," Ju grumbled under her breath. "Or I am gonna be *so* mad at you and Mommy."

Joseph's face flushed. "I'm sorry, was there anything else, Alice?" he asked, clearly embarrassed and eager to end the conversation.

"Yes, sir," she said. "There's a package for you down at the front desk, and the courier is insisting you must sign for it yourself. I assure you, I tried to tell him that I was authorized to receive it for you, but he wouldn't..."

"Did we scan it?"

"We did, sir. It's clean."

"No matter, then" Joseph said, waving his hand. "We'll be down in just a few minutes. Thank you for your time, Alice."

Alice nodded. "You're welcome, Mr. Cho. You two have a good lunch, okay?" She smiled and waved at Ju, who pretended not to see her, feigning interest in the sculpture once again. "Alright then," she said cheerfully, taking her exit through the front door and disappearing back into the hallway.

Joseph frowned at his daughter. "Now, that wasn't very nice of you, was it Ju?"

"What?" his daughter said as innocently as possible, avoiding eye contact.

"The way you treated Alice just then."

Ju opened her mouth to protest, but decided it wasn't really worth the energy it would require to argue the point. She shrugged, hiding a sly smile from her father.

Joseph stared at her for a few more seconds, then gave up, focusing once again on the papers adorning his desk. He had learned long ago that it wasn't worth arguing a point with his daughter, especially when it came to her behavior—or *mis*behavior, as was typically the case. Just like her mother, she was doggedly determined to win in life, every single moment of every single day, as if she were a constant contestant. He often justified his shortcomings as a father by reassuring himself that she would one day make a fantastic successor to the family business.

But when it came to raising a spirited, seven-year-old girl, he had to admit to himself that he would much rather wrestle with a hostile corporate acquisition any day.

o   o   o

"Is there a problem here?"

Megan peered over the bank counter at the squat woman and frowned. "Are you being serious right now?"

The older woman, stuffed into a mustard yellow pantsuit that was at least one size too small for her, didn't flinch. She'd been an assistant manager at Shield Bank and Trust for the past eighteen months, and she wasn't afraid to speak her mind. Especially when it came to dealing with a snotty college kid.

"I am absolutely serious, Ms. Loften. When one of my employees summons me from my office and informs me that we have an unruly customer—"

"Unruly!"

"—then it's my job to get to the bottom of things," the woman continued, undeterred. "So I repeat myself: is there a problem here?"

Megan's jaw dropped in shock. She could hardly believe what she was hearing. She had just attended a fantastic, three-day PETA seminar in Las Vegas, and on a whim decided to get some traveling cash before heading back home. At first she had been hesitant to make a withdrawal at a bank in the middle of a mall. Based on past experience, her having cash on hand and an endless array of shopping stops made for a lethal combination. Now she realized that blowing her budget was the least of her headaches.

"Look, lady…"

"Mrs. Simmerts."

"Whatever," Megan snapped, waving her hand. "You should know that I've been a happy member of Shield Bank and Trust for the past fifteen years—"

"We've been in business for ten," Mrs. Simmerts said, a triumphant smile creeping across her face.

Megan blinked, stunned at having her "loyal customer" ruse shredded so fast. "Listen. All I wanted to do was come in here, make a quick withdrawal, and get back on the road. I wasn't even *having* a 'problem' until Bambi there couldn't get my account number right. Even after three attempts."

"It's Barbara," Mrs. Simmerts growled as the thin girl behind her stared at the floor in shame.

"Barbara…Bambi…*I really don't care what you call her.* I just want to get my money and get out." She backed away from the counter a few inches and conjured up the most saccharin smile she could. "If you please," she said, trying to hide the blazing fury behind her eyes.

The shorter woman stared back at her, unmoving. Finally she stepped up to the computer terminal and started typing. "Fine. May I have your bank card?"

"I already gave it to Bambi," Megan muttered in frustration, closing her eyes and rubbing the bridge of her nose.

Simmerts shot her a look. Then she turned around to face the girl standing behind her. "Barbara?"

"I…I gave it to you back at your office…" a wide-eyed Barbara squeaked back.

Mrs. Simmerts stared at her, her face a mixture of contempt and impatience.

"Fine," she said, turning around to face Megan, "Ms. Loften, if you would please step aside so we can help the next customer, I will personally retrieve your card from my office, and we'll see if we can't sort this out as quickly as possible, shall we?"

"No."

"Excuse me?" the older woman asked, surprised.

Megan leaned in closer. "I said 'no,'" she repeated.

Mrs. Simmerts frowned. "What do you mean, 'no'? No *what?*"

Megan crossed her arms and placed them on counter. "No, *ma'am.* As in, 'no, I won't let you brush me aside like an unwanted stepchild while you help the *next* customer.' I'm not moving until you get back. So I suggest your hurry your butt up a bit."

The woman glared at Megan. "I don't think I like your tone."

"And I don't think I *care* what you think, lady. You've already wasted a good fifteen minutes of my life, time that I'll never, *ever* get back. So if you don't mind?" She gestured toward the direction the woman had originated from. "I'd *really* like to get my money, get the hell out of Vegas, and go home."

The pudgy woman's face flushed red, and Megan watched in amusement as her mouth opened to say something, then snapped shut. Without saying another word, the yellow-clad manager stormed off behind the counter, a petrified Barbara fluttering in her wake.

Megan closed her eyes and started rubbing the bridge of her nose again. She sighed deeply. "Unbelievable," she muttered to herself.

"Is there a problem here?" a male voice asked from behind her. Megan spun around, mentally preparing to hash it out with yet another bank employee. Instead she found herself face-to-face with an attractive guy in hiking gear. His friend, equally good-looking and similarly dressed, stood close behind him, smiling.

Megan looked at them, confused.

The first guy's smiled broadened, and he chuckled. "I'm sorry...I was just making fun of Mrs. Crumpet, there." He jutted his chin toward the teller booth. "Apparently she doesn't subscribe to the mantra of 'the customer is always right.'"

Megan smiled. Finally, someone understood what was going on from her perspective! Plus, it didn't hurt that the guy was actually kind of cute. "No kidding," she said, smiling at first and then shrugging. "Look, I'm sorry you guys have to wait so long, I just…"

"Ah, don't worry about it," he said, waving his hand. "I would've done the same thing."

"Really?"

"Totally. I swear."

"Well, thank you," she said. "I appreciate it."

He held out his hand. "Welcome to Vegas, by the way. I'm Dan. This is my roommate, Scott."

"Hey there!" Scott gushed, a little too enthusiastically.

She shook Dan's hand. "Megan," she said. "Bought some new camping gear, did we?" She gestured at their backpacks, the price tags still dangling from the zippers.

"Yeah," Dan said. "Actually, we're just going on a day hike tomorrow morning—"

"Wanna come?" Scott interjected, grinning at her.

"Ah, no. Thank you. I'm afraid I'm not much of a nature girl," she said. "Plus, I'm really hoping to catch my flight back to St. Louis tonight, drink a few glasses of wine, and cuddle on the couch with my cat. Assuming I'm able to get my money in *this* century, that is." She rolled her eyes, shaking her head in mock disapproval. In Dan and Scott's eyes, it only served to multiply her cuteness quotient a hundredfold.

"Hey, what's the hold up? I got places to be," someone yelled from the line behind them. Megan looked past Dan and Scott at the other people standing behind them: two large, overweight men dressed in the most garish tropical tourist getups she'd ever seen, a middle-aged guy in a baseball cap casually peeling an orange, and behind him a skinny Santa, shifting on his feet with eyes that said he was clearly annoyed.

Megan looked at the Santa and frowned, then she remembered Christmas was less than a week away. The weather in Las Vegas had been so warm the past few days she'd almost completely forgotten it was still winter in the rest of the country.

Dan glared at the tourist who had complained. Despite the intimidating size of the older man, he felt compelled to step up in a valiant attempt to defend Megan's honor. "Yo, what's your problem, dude?"

The man smiled and leaned in closer to him. "My 'problem' is I got other things to do today than stand around while some bimbo hijacks the teller line."

"Hey, maybe you should just back off a bit, huh?" Dan barked back. "It's not like it's her fault they're so freaking slow, now is it?"

The man started to take a step toward him when the other tourist, massive arms straining under his radioactive yellow Hawaiian shirt, reached over and pulled him back.

"Tanner. Man, just let it go, okay?" he said. "This isn't the place to make a scene or nothin', remember?" Tanner looked at him, and his friend slowly shook his head in disapproval. "Not here," he whispered, frowning.

Tanner glowered at him, then looked back at Dan and Megan, sneering. "Whatever," he muttered, shaking his head and staring out the lobby windows at the mall patrons outside.

"I'm really sorry for my friend here," the other guy

apologized to Megan. "He's been kind of tightly strung lately. He'll be fine. Sorry for the...um..." He frowned, trying to find the right words. "Well, we're just sorry is all..." he shrugged, giving up.

Megan didn't respond. She stared at the two men as they returned to their places in line and shook her head in disbelief. *Unbelievable*, she thought. Up until today she had thoroughly enjoyed her first taste of Vegas. Now she just wanted to put as much distance between her and the impatient asylum wannabes that surrounded her.

With the exception of Dan and Scott, of course. Sure, they looked like granola-munching dweebs decked out in their outdoor gear in the middle of a bank lobby, but they were cute, and they stuck up for her. Despite the perpetual rudeness of the past few minutes, Megan had to conclude that chivalry was alive and kicking in Las Vegas.

o   o   o

The elevator lurched to a stop at the lobby level, the subtle ding of a bell announcing their arrival as the doors opened for Ju and her father. Even at seven Ju still loved riding in her father's private elevator. The privacy and plush carpet weren't even the best parts. No, the *best* part was when the doors opened and she saw the shocked and surprised looks on the faces of the unsuspecting people outside.

Because from their perspective there were only *two* elevators: those they saw directly in front of them. Her father's executive elevator had been designed so securely that the doors were expertly hidden behind the expensive, Corian tile work adorning the lobby. Only when he arrived did the two gigantic slabs slip away from the wall and silently slid to the side, revealing the special guests inside.

They stepped out onto the carpet and Ju turned around, relishing the shocked look frozen on the face of an old lady to her left. Grinning, she watched the elevator doors close, followed by the walls, sliding seamlessly back into their previous positions. Ju looked up at her father.

"That is *so* cool," she said.

"I know it is," he said, smiling at her. "You remind me every time."

She shrugged as they walked toward the lobby. "I can't help it. It's just so *cool*! I want one!"

"You want what? An elevator to play with?"

"Yes!"

"Darling, you can use this one anytime you visit me at the office…"

"No, Dad. I want my *own*," Ju whined.

Joseph sighed. "Very well. Perhaps we can talk about this some other time?"

"Whatever," Ju said, sulking as she stared at her feet.

He didn't give her the satisfaction of throwing a fit. "Thank you. Now, Daddy has to go over to the desk to take care of something. It should only take a minute, so you stay right here, okay?"

"Whatever," she repeated in a sing-song voice, not looking up.

Choosing not to indulge her impetuousness any longer than absolutely necessary, Joseph swiftly walked toward the offices behind the teller booths.

Ju watched him leave, realizing her pouting had had no effect and she no longer had an audience. Her frown faded and she looked up, casually scanning the lobby. People watching had always been one of her favorite pastimes. Despite her self-assertiveness and a penchant for speaking her mind, Ju liked to consider herself an introvert by nature. At least, that was her only explanation for her occasional desire to fade into the shadows and experience life as a silent observer.

She wasn't disappointed. Today's patrons were proving to be very colorful in every way imaginable.

Waiting in one of the teller lines was the strangest collection of people Ju could have ever assembled. At the front of the line was a girl that Ju estimated was in college, or her early twenties at the most. She was tall and pretty and had a nice smile. Ju liked her instantly. Behind her stood two younger guys wearing tan hiking boots and two huge backpacks strapped to their backs.

Nature lovers, Ju thought to herself, chuckling.

They were obviously having some kind of an argument with the two men behind them, wearing the stereotypical Vegas tourist gear: ultra-bright floral shirts, overstuffed fanny packs, and shorts that showed far too much pasty leg than should have been legally allowed. They even had sunglasses on — in the middle of a lobby *in a mall*.

Ju shook her head in disapproval. "Idiots," she muttered.

She shifted her focus on the guy in a baseball cap behind them, casually eating an orange. She watched him carefully remove a segment and expertly toss it up into his mouth. She wondered if he was eating the seeds and all, and suddenly felt an intense desire to eat one herself.

Standing behind the orange eater, however, was the most surprising person of the lot. Santa Claus himself. Or rather, one of Santa's super-skinny helpers, Ju guessed. The guy was so tall his suit didn't even fit properly, riding up on his legs at least four inches, enough so Ju would see his leg hairs from where she stood.

"So gross," she said, disgusted. "Fa-la-la-la *fail.*"

Ju looked toward where her father had left. He was engaged in an intense conversation with a short, squat mustard lady who kept pointing toward the teller station. He was thoroughly distracted, not even glancing in her direction. Ju smiled, looking back to the Santa.

She was going to have some fun.

Casually walking across the lobby, she stood right beside Santa and smiled. He didn't notice her whatsoever, but was glancing over his shoulder at the bank entrance, watching one of his holiday counterparts ringing the bell just outside the doors. Ju cleared her throat loudly to get his attention, but he still didn't notice her.

"Hey Santa!" she said loudly.

His head spun around and he glared at the line of people waiting ahead of him, then down at Ju. She thought he looked extremely nervous or annoyed. Or both.

"Oh, hey there," he said looking down at her, then away, staring at the line of tellers.

Ju snapped her fingers. "Hey. Down here."

He brought his attention back her, his eyes boring into her. "What do you want?"

"I have a question," Ju blurted out. Out of the corner of her eye she noticed the two tourist guys had stopped arguing with the college dudes and were now focused entirely on her. She grinned inside. Humiliating people was always fun, but it was much more entertaining if you had an audience around to watch.

Santa shifted on his feet and shrugged. "Okay, little girl. What's your question?"

"Where's your gut?"

She watched his eyebrows crease. "Where's my what?"

"Your gut," she said, pointing to his midsection. "You're not very fat for a Santa, you know."

"Yeah, I guess those low-fat candy canes kinda gave me the runs, so…"

"What?" Ju asked, confused.

"I…I been hitting the gym a lot lately," Santa countered, changing his tactic. "You know, running on the treadmill and stuff?" He jogged in place for a few seconds, then stopped and patted his belly. "See? Exercise is good for you. You should try it."

Ju's eyes narrowed. "What did you just say to me?" she seethed. This holiday moron obviously had no clue who she was, or whose bank he was in.

Santa held up his hands in innocent protest. "Hey, I'm just sayin' you look like you could probably lay off the Christmas cookies yourself, huh? Know what

I'm sayin'?" He patted his belly again, laughing.

Ju was infuriated.

Without hesitating, she stepped forward and swung her fist at his stomach. He lurched backwards and laughed at her. "Whoa, slow down there, sumo. You might hurt yourself, there," he chuckled.

Ju's face shifted to a deeper shade of crimson as she felt the uncontrollable fury bubble up inside of her. Cursing at him in her native Korean, Ju swung at him with her other hand. This time he didn't try to dodge it. Instead he reached out and caught her arm in mid-swing, wrenching it tightly behind her back.

Ju screamed.

Santa reached behind him and removed a gun from the back of his waistband. He pressed the barrel into her temple hard enough to make her stop screaming. Everyone in the lobby stared at them in shock, unmoving, unable to determine if this was an act or if they were actually witnessing Santa Claus take a little girl hostage at gunpoint.

A second later there was a loud gunshot from the entrance, and out of the corner of her eye Ju saw the second Santa from outside the bank standing over the guard, gun in hand. She watched as he pulled the trigger again, the guard's body jumping with the impact. A moment later the Santa dropped to one knee, reached into his oversized black bag and slapped a large bike lock through the door handles, locking everyone inside.

"Everybody down on the ground!" he yelled, spinning around and swinging his gun toward the lobby in a wide arc. "On the ground! Now!" He raised the gun and shot once into the ceiling, evoking a series of shouts and screams as people dove down to the cold tile floor, covering their heads with shaking hands.

"You heard the man!" the Santa holding Ju yelled. "Kiss the ground! Do it now!!"

Everyone who had been waiting in line dropped instantly to the ground, with the exception of one of the tourists, his bright yellow shirt branding him as a distinct target against the muted silvers and greys of the lobby decor.

"Hey man," he said nervously, holding his hands up in front of him. "Don't do anything crazy, now." He looked down at Ju who had her eyes shut tight. "Just...just let the girl go, huh? She didn't do nothin'..."

"Are you serious?" Santa snarled at him, gun extended. "For one, why the hell are you wearing sunglasses inside? Is there something wrong with you?"

"I'm sorry," the man said, reaching up to remove his glasses. "I guess—"

"Shut up," Santa said, aiming at his head. "Don't answer that."

"Okay..."

"Secondly, you *do* realize that she took a swing at me first, right?"

"I know, but—"

"And finally, *I'm pointing a freaking gun at your head!*"

"Okay, okay..." he said, putting his arms down slowly.

"So GET ON THE GROUND!" Santa yelled furiously. *"Now!"*

The older man slunk down to his stomach and lay prostrate on the floor, hands outstretched above him. He stared up at the Santa, a look of defeat in his eyes.

"And don't look at me," Santa snapped at him. "Unless you wanna get shot." The tourist complied, turning his head the other way and laying it on the floor. He sighed deeply.

Santa spun around, tightly clutching Ju's twisted wrist as she whimpered in the background. "Time?" he yelled to the other Santa by the door.

"Two minutes, seventeen seconds!"

He nodded.

"Joseph Cho!" he yelled at the teller stations. "I know you're down here, and I know you can hear me! You have one minute to show yourself or your daughter's gonna have an awfully hard time playing piano next week!" He twisted Ju's arm higher behind her and forced her to her knees. Pushing the gun into the center of the back of her hand, he nestled it painfully into the bones.

"Daddy!" Ju screamed, tears streaming down her face.

"Fifty-seven, fifty-six, fifty-five..."

"DADDY!"

"Fifty-four, fifty-three..."

"Two minutes, two seconds!" the other Santa yelled.

The first Santa cursed under his breath. "You're wasting my time," he yelled. "*Ten...nine...eight...*"

"*DADDY!*" Ju shrieked even louder than before.

"*Seven...*"

"Stop!"

Santa smiled under his itchy beard as he watched Joseph Cho step around the corner of a nearby wall, hands raised. "Now that's more like it," he whispered to himself.

"Please. Let my daughter go," Joseph pleaded, gesturing to Ju. "She's innocent."

"She may be innocent, but you know what? She's also the rudest kid I've ever met," Santa said, shaking her enough to elicit a renewed stream of tears.

"Daddy..." she whispered, looking up into his eyes. Joseph saw how terrified she was, and his heart twisted inside of him at her anguish.

"I have what you want here," he said, reaching behind the counter.

"Watch it, old man!" Santa barked, raising the gun to Ju's head.

Joseph moved slowly, his left hand still raised, and pulled a large, black duffel bag into view. It was unzipped, and even from across the room, Santa could see it was packed with stacks of bills.

"Three hundred thousand dollars," Joseph said when he set it down between them. "Please. Take it and leave. I promise I won't pursue you or ever press charges."

Santa snickered. "Yeah, well, thanks...but no thanks. I'd rather not get a faceful of dye pack when I'm driving off into the sunset."

"No dye packs," Joseph said calmly. "No tracers or trackers of any kind. Just free money for you and your friend." He nodded to the other Santa by the door.

"You'll forgive me if I don't take your word for it."

"I never lie," Joseph said, unwavering.

"Minute and a half!" the second Santa shouted. "Come on already!"

"Please!" Joseph pleaded, taking two steps toward his daughter. "Take the money! Just don't hurt my daughter!"

"Relax, we're not here to kill your daughter," Santa said, shaking his head. Then his face hardened and he slowly pulled the gun away from her head and pointed it directly as Joseph's. "We're here to kill you."

Even as he pulled the trigger, what Santa saw next filled him with a sudden mixture of confusion and dread. They were the last two emotions he ever felt.

Joseph smiled at him.

The loud blast of the gunshot filled the room with a renewed wave of panic and hysteria. The back of Santa's head suddenly exploded, showering the patrons on the ground with blood, brains, and fragments of bone. He slumped over onto Ju's back and slid to the floor beside her in a heap.

Ju screamed.

Her eyes darted at the people surrounding her, watched as the guy in the baseball cap reached up and wiped something red and wet off of his cheek. The pretty girl and her boyfriends stared back at her, frozen in shock and disbelief.

Joseph ran over to his daughter and knelt beside her, wrapping her in his arms and burying her face in his shoulder. He glared at the second Santa, who was now staring down at his partner, dead and bleeding all over the tile floor.

"What the hell!" he screamed, waving the gun around the room, searching for the shooter. "Show yourself! Or I'll shoot them! I swear I'll do it!" He ran over to where Joseph and Ju were crouched on the floor and pointed his gun at them.

"Please! Take the money and leave!" Joseph shouted.

"Call them off!" Santa Two yelled, the gun shaking in his hand. "Do it now! Or I'll—"

"I can't! There's no one to call off!" Joseph insisted "Please! Take the money! Run!"

Santa stared over at the bag of cash, clearly thinking it over for a few seconds. Finally he looked back at Joseph and nodded. "Fine. I'll take your money. But I gotta finish the job first."

"Please, you don't have to do this…"

"What? And spend the rest of my life lookin' over my shoulder? No way."

"I promise you, I won't try to find you."

Santa laughed. "It ain't *you* I'm worried about," he said, pointing the gun at Joseph's forehead. "Say good-bye to Daddy, girl."

"Daddy!" Ju said, clutching his hand.

"It's alright," Joseph said quietly, staring at the barrel of the gun. "Ju. Close your eyes, please. Do it now." He gave one last, saddened look at the man in the Santa suit, shook his head in disappointment and closed his eyes.

There was the sound of a second shot, and Joseph heard more shouts and screams fill the lobby, followed by the muted noise of a body falling to the floor. He waited for another few seconds before he opened his eyes, savoring the moment.

When he looked down he saw the lifeless body of the second Santa lying next to the first, a steady stream of blood now seeping out of the neat bullet hole in the center of his forehead. Joseph rose to his feet, shaking his head sadly.

"What a waste," he whispered to himself, reaching down and lifting his daughter to her feet. Stepping over the body, he carried Ju across the lobby toward the back offices.

Two hours later...

Ju sat next to her father in the back of the limousine on the way home, nuzzling her face into his neck. She inhaled his scent, a faint mixture of aspen and vanilla, his favorite as long as she'd known him. He slowly stroked her forearm with his hand, each pass filling her with another sense of peace and safety.

She had stopped crying shortly after the police had arrived at the bank, bottling up her emotions as they interviewed the witnesses with an endless array of questions. The pretty college girl had waved at her absently before leaving. It made Ju feel happy for a few seconds, before the anger and pain of what had happened eclipsed her mind again.

"Quite the day, wasn't it?" her father said quietly, looking down at her. He had rarely seen his daughter rendered so speechless, and it worried him. Protecting himself wasn't the issue. It had never been an issue, and never would be. Still, he couldn't stop worrying about his family. These two had failed in today's assassination attempt. There would undoubtedly be others, and he would be ready for them. He wouldn't always be beside Ju to protect her from the threats outside. Maybe it was time he reached out for help.

"Perhaps," he said, staring out the window, "we should postpone your party until next week?"

Ju sat up quickly. "No! Please! I've been *so* looking forward to it! Please?" She looked at him with wide, pleading eyes.

Joseph looked back at her, his heart melting. "Honey, are you sure? Perhaps you should take more time to…recover…from today."

"Please, Daddy. I'll be fine," she said, placing her head back into his neck. "I promise."

"Well, if you think so, then—"

"I do," Ju interrupted. "Besides, I don't want to wait another week to get my pony." She looked up at him, trying to gauge his reaction.

Joseph smiled at her. "Mmm-hmmm," he said, maintaining a perfect poker face.

"I think I'm going to love my pony," she mused, putting her head back. "I promise," she whispered.

"And *I* think that you will be pleasantly surprised with the birthday gifts you'll get tomorrow," he said, smiling. "I promise."

Author's Note

Without question, this was one of the most difficult, high-concept short stories I've ever written. The idea was simple: write an original story using a cast of characters featured in *Snapdragon* up to this point. I think I was inspired by J.A. Konrath's novel *The List*, (or was it *Haunted House?*) that wove a new story featuring previous characters. (Todd Travis did it in *The Living and The Dead* as well.) I figured it would be a blast to try.

I was right.

Granted, it took more work than I typically invest in a short story. I had to come up with a public location, decide which characters to include, and how to reveal them to the reader, as well as rewrite some of the scenes and dialogue in the previous stories to make them mesh better, but it was nonetheless a ton of fun.

I also love the idea of hiding the story at the end of the collection, uncredited in the table of contents. You've spent your hard-earned cash on my book when there were a ton of other alternatives to choose from. The least I could do is give you something special back in return.

Thank you so much for reading!

- Jack

DEAR READER,

I just want to thank you once again for reading these stories. I hope you enjoyed the characters I've created, and will be back for more when I release my second anthology next year.

If you did enjoy Snapdragon, please consider showing your support by posting a review at one of the various online review sites (*Amazon, Goodreads, iBooks, etc.*). These websites work on algorithms, so the more people who gush about my books? The more they'll be recommended for other readers.

More reviews? More readers. More readers? More fans who will clamor to get the next fix of fiction. It's too easy to simply pay for a glowing review. I'd rather just come right out and ask you, a loyal reader, to voice your actual opinion.

Again, thank you so much for your time and support!

- Jack

ABOUT THE AUTHOR

Jack Kardiac was born in Siloam Springs, Arkansas and grew up in Tulsa, Oklahoma. He was raised on a steady diet of comic books, Twilight Zone episodes, and Alfred Hitchcock paperbacks. He watches *Die Hard* every Christmas and *Peter Jackson's King Kong* every summer. In reality, he likes to make people think, laugh, and change the world for the better. When he writes, he enjoys having people desperately running for their lives. Preferably from a giant monster.

Jack currently lives in the remote jungles of Indonesia where he teaches Creative Writing to young, impressionable minds.

And yes, he has a twin brother.

13 Savory Short Stories...
...with a Dash of Darkness.

Indulge your craving for flavor-filled short stories with *Death & Peaches*, a tantalizing fusion of thrills, chills and hand-picked, selective surprises. Painstakingly crafted over many years with the precision of a master chef, each story delivers a delectable blend of spicy suspense, juicy tenderness, and a heaping helping of humor.

Haven't you waited long enough? Sink your teeth into the sinister sweetness that is *Death & Peaches* — guaranteed to satisfy the most sophisticated literary palette, from first bite to last.

Available now! So why wait? Get your slice today!